1914

. . . Susan slid the photograph
out of the frame to have a closer look.
And then, right into her lap, as if inviting
itself to be read, dropped the letter.
Bea's letter. The *secret* letter. *Tick-tick,
tick-tick,* went the clock. A horn beeped
down in the street. Susan's pulse beat
in her throat. She unfolded the
letter and began to read. . . .

SECRETS ON 26TH STREET

❧

by
Elizabeth McDavid Jones

Printed in the United States of America.
99 00 01 02 03 04 RRD 10 9 8 7 6 5 4 3 2 1

History Mysteries™ and American Girl™
are trademarks of Pleasant Company.

PERMISSIONS & PICTURE CREDITS

WESTERN UNION is a registered service mark owned by
Western Union Holdings, Inc., and is used by permission.

The following organizations have generously given permission to reprint
illustrations contained in "A Peek into the Past": p. 139 — Schlesinger Library, Radcliffe
College; pp. 140-141 — State Historical Society of Wisconsin (ad; Anthony/Stanton); Corbis/Hulton-
Deutsch Collection, #HU002179 (Mrs. Pankhurst); National Woman's Party, Washington, DC (jail);
pp. 142-143 — National Woman's Party (Alice Paul); Corbis/Bettmann, #BE041000 (three women);
Museum of the City of New York, acc. #47.225.21 ("Yes" button), #47.225.11 ("Votes" button); photo-
graph by Lewis W. Hine, courtesy George Eastman House, Rochester, NY, #GEH 34226 (factory);
Library of Congress, acc. #C4 2654 DLC (laundry); Corbis, #IH157143 (doorway); pp. 144-145 —
Picture Collection, The Branch Libraries, The New York Public Library (Tammany Hall drawing);
Library of Congress, neg. #62-90463 (parade) and
neg. #C4-2996 DLC (program); Culver Pictures (speaker); Corbis, #IH190363 (voters);
Museum of the City of New York, acc. #47.225.16 (button).

Cover and Map Illustrations: Robert Sauber
Line Art: Greg Dearth
Editor: Peg Ross
Art Direction: Jane Varda
Design: Laura Moberly and Kimberly Strother

Library of Congress Cataloging-in-Publication Data

Jones, Elizabeth McDavid, 1958-
Secrets on 26th Street / by Elizabeth McDavid Jones.
p. cm. — (History mysteries)
"American girl."
Summary: In New York City in 1914, eleven-year-old Susan encounters a mystery
through an independent-minded female boarder and becomes involved
in the growing suffrage movement.
ISBN 1-56247-816-8 (hardcover) ISBN 1-56247-760-9 (pbk.)
[1. Women — Suffrage Fiction. 2. Sex role Fiction.
3. Irish Americans Fiction. 4. New York (N.Y.) Fiction. 5. Mystery and detective stories.]
I. Title II. Title: Secrets on Twenty-Sixth Street. III. Series.
PZ7.J6855 Se 1999 [Fic]—dc21 99-29899 CIP

To my husband, Rick,
and my children, Mandy, Lindsay,
Whitney, and Michael

TABLE OF CONTENTS

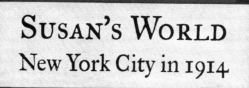

SUSAN'S WORLD
New York City in 1914

Chelsea Piers

Hudson River

Suffrage rally

26th Street

CHAPTER I
THREATS

Patience.

As Susan O'Neal stood on the sidewalk in the drizzle, waiting for Helen, she thought having to be patient was the absolute hardest thing about being a big sister. If it wasn't waiting for little Lucy to painstakingly button her own shoes when Susan could have done it in a flash, then it was waiting for Helen to finish picking at her oatmeal in the morning so Susan could get the dishes washed up and she and Helen could get to school. Susan knew Mum needed her more than ever since Dad died last year, but sometimes it felt like no other eleven-year-old in Chelsea, maybe in all of New York City, had more chores than she did. Sometimes Susan thought it would be nice just to do what *she* wanted for a change.

Like now. It was cold for September, and all of Chelsea was gray—gray like the granite curbstones, gray like the factory smoke, gray like the Hudson River that formed

the neighborhood's western border. The rain fell gray
on the sidewalks and gray on the rooftops, gray on the
streets and on the umbrellas of hurrying pedestrians.

It was a day for hurrying, Susan thought, not for
poking along, waiting for little sisters. What Susan wanted
to do was to rush home from school and curl up in front
of the stove with the novel her teacher had assigned her
to read. Susan couldn't wait to get home and dive in, for
just an *hour* or so, before she had to start chores. There'd
be no time to read later, that was for sure. Tonight the
new boarder was coming, and Mum had to work late. She
was depending on Susan to tidy up the flat and have dinner
ready when the boarder arrived at six.

Susan knew if she didn't hurry Helen along now, there
wouldn't be a *minute* to read, much less an hour. It was
already a quarter past four, and they'd walked only six
blocks, little more than halfway home to their building on
26th Street. Helen was being an absolute snail, and it was
all Susan could do to keep from losing her temper.

"Helen, come on," Susan said. "You've stopped to look
at posters at every movie house on the avenue." When
Dad was alive, he would sometimes give the girls money
to see a Saturday matinee. There was no money for shows
now, though, and Helen sorely missed them.

Helen acted as if she hadn't even heard Susan. "Oh,
Susie, isn't she beautiful?" She was staring dreamily at a
poster featuring Mary Pickford. Helen loved the romantic

pictures Pickford starred in, where the handsome hero always fell in love with her and they lived happily ever after. Susan preferred exciting westerns or the comedies with Charlie Chaplin.

Susan backed up to look at the poster Helen was mooning over. She wrinkled up her nose in disgust. It looked like the actress was once again playing a damsel in distress. Susan wished that just once Mary Pickford would catch the bank robbers herself instead of depending on the handsome hero to do it.

Susan turned her head sideways to try to see what Helen saw in the willowy, golden-haired Pickford. "I suppose she's pretty enough, but I think Mum is prettier. Mum's eyes have more life in them."

At least they used to, Susan thought. Before Dad died and Mum had so many bills to worry about.

"I'm going to be a star just like Mary Pickford some-day." Helen turned from the poster and strode forward with an eight-year-old's confidence that her dreams would come true. "You wait and see."

Susan picked up Helen's book strap from the side-walk where Helen had dropped it and scrambled after her. "A redheaded, Irish Mary Pickford?" Susan teased. She knew Helen's dream was impossible, though she wouldn't say so to Helen. After all, Susan remembered what it was like to be eight years old, even though it seemed like centuries ago.

"They have wigs, you know," Helen said huffily. "And I could change my name so no one would know I'm Irish."

"What would you change it to?"

Helen glanced at the shop window they were passing. *Rutger's and Jefferson's Clothing for Men.* Swelling her chest, she said regally, "I'll be Lillian Jefferson."

"It's a grand name," Susan said, "though you've stolen the whole of it. I don't think Mum will mind you using 'Lillian'—even though it's the name *she* picked out back when she dreamed of acting in vaudeville—but Mr. Jefferson might object. When you become rich and famous, that is."

"I'll be so rich, I'll split it with him."

Susan laughed. She was thinking, though, about her own dream for the future. It wasn't a career in show business she wanted, but it was nearly as impossible. That's why she never spoke of it, not even to Mum. Why, it was just as silly for Susan to dream of going to City College to study literature as it was for Helen to dream of being Mary Pickford, or Mum to dream of performing on the vaudeville stage. Who ever heard of a poor Irish girl from the tenements going to college? Most of the older girls Susan knew had gone straight to work in the factories after finishing grammar school. If she was lucky, Susan thought, she'd end up like her friend Russell Cochran's older sister: a chambermaid in a mansion on Fifth Avenue, wearing an apron and picking up other people's dirty laundry. The thought depressed her immensely.

The sky darkened with Susan's mood; the rain picked up, and the wind changed direction and blew the rain into their faces. Some people scurried to get out of the downpour, hailing cabs or huddling under awnings. Susan and Helen simply hurried faster along their way—past Kelly's Stables and the blacksmith shop beside it, past Kosler's butcher shop, past the secondhand store where Mum bought most of their clothes. In the empty lot next to the store, a pile of rubbish, blown by the wind, swirled into the air, danced gaily for a moment, then dropped back to earth.

The scene sent a wave of restlessness rushing over Susan. *I might as well dream of wearing diamonds on my toes,* she thought glumly, *for my dream'll never happen.* She plunged right through a puddle and ignored Helen's scolding. They were almost home now—in front of Murray's Tavern on the corner of 28th and Tenth.

Susan glanced up at two women standing in front of the tavern holding signs. The printing on their signs had faded in the rain, but Susan could still make out the large, bold letters: VOTES FOR WOMEN.

Suffragists. Every now and then, they would show up in the neighborhood with petitions for people to sign. Sometimes they would stand on soapboxes on the sidewalk and talk about things Susan mostly didn't understand, like "enfranchisement of women." Most folks didn't pay them much mind. Susan remembered one suffragist very well, though. Some of the tough boys had pelted her with rotten tomatoes as she was speaking, but she'd stood her ground. With tomato running down her face, she'd shouted them down and dared them to throw another one.

Susan had thought if that woman wasn't Irish, she should be, and for the first time it had made Susan curious about suffrage. Soon afterward, there was a suffrage parade down Fifth Avenue, and Susan had wanted to go. But Mum wouldn't take her; she said she didn't have twenty cents to spend on carfare for such a lost cause.

"Why don't those ladies go in out of the rain like everyone else?" Helen asked.

The yellow chrysanthemums on the suffragists' hats were drooping in the rain. Susan shrugged in answer to Helen's question. "I dunno, Helen. They're suffragists. Too stubborn to give up, I wager. Figure they'll get their way if they keep hounding the men to give them the vote. But whatever they do, it won't change our lives."

Only two more blocks to home, but Susan was feeling so gloomy, it seemed the two blocks stretched forever. At 27th and Eleventh Avenue, a newsboy was screaming out headlines about the war in Europe. Susan knew that England and France were fighting Germany and Austria. The newspapers were always full of war news—battles and troop movements. But the war felt far away to Susan, and she'd gotten so used to the headlines she scarcely noticed them anymore. "Read all about it," the newsboy cried. "German spy caught in Paris!"

This particular headline, though, grabbed Susan's attention for an instant—she had just finished reading an exciting book about Nathan Hale, a Revolutionary War spy. But the smell of D'Attilio's Bakery reminded her that Mum had asked them to stop on their way home from school and buy bread for dinner.

Helen drew in a deep whiff. "Oooh, the bread smells good," she said. "Since Mum didn't tell us what kind to get, does that mean we can choose?"

"I guess it does," said Susan. The thought of choosing among D'Attilio's delicious loaves—rye, wheat, pumpernickel—chased away Susan's gloom. "Depends on what he'll give us for a nickel." A nickel was only enough for day-old bread, but it was all Mum could spare, and she'd told Susan to try to talk D'Attilio into a fresh loaf. "If we can't feed this boarder decently," Mum had said, "we can't hope to keep her, and we have *got* to keep her. She's our only hope to make this month's rent." Susan couldn't forget how Mum's eyes had burned with intensity. She reached in her pocket and fingered the nickel's cool hardness. She hoped she could live up to Mum's faith in her.

The bell above the door tinkled as the girls pushed their way into the crowded bakery. While Helen wandered around looking at pastries and breads in the display cases, Susan waited in line behind their neighbor Mrs. Flynn. Mum always said Mrs. Flynn, who lived on the fifth floor right above the O'Neals, was better than the *Times* for giving news of the neighborhood; she seemed to know everything that happened on the block.

At the moment, Mrs. Flynn was trying to hold on to her twin boys while balancing the baby on her hip. "How's your mum holding up, lass? Last time I saw her she was pale as the moon. I'm hoping she's not ailing." Mrs. Flynn's eyes showed concern.

Susan didn't know how to put into words her fears about Mum. Mum was looking so thin lately, and dark circles had appeared under her eyes, no doubt from exhaustion and worry. Even though Mum worked at the shipping office down on the docks twelve hours a day, six days a week, she was four months behind on the rent, and the landlord had been pressing Mum for payment. "Well, she's not exactly ailing," Susan said. "But she hasn't been herself."

"Coming down with something, is she? I wager she's been working herself too hard, coming in after dark every evening. God love her, she never sees the sun, does she? Well, you tell her I'll be by real soon. Tell her I'll be by."

Susan promised.

Then Mrs. Flynn's voice took on a serious tone. "You lassies lock your door tonight, y'hear me? There've been break-ins on 27th, right behind us. They're saying it's the

Jimmy Curley Gang, fresh out of Sing Sing prison, the lot of 'em. Lock your doors tight."

Susan breathed a little faster. She'd heard stories about Jimmy Curley and his hoodlums shaking down businesses and pushcart peddlers for money, threatening to poison their horses, or worse, if they didn't pay up. Helen was lingering in front of the pastry display, but she was staring straight at Mrs. Flynn, and Susan was sure she'd heard. Grand. Now Helen would have nightmares for a week.

Before Mrs. Flynn could say more, the customer at the counter turned around, and Susan groaned. It was Lester Barrow. He was the powerful district leader of Tammany Hall, the circle of Democratic politicians that ran the city. He also happened to be the O'Neals' landlord. With his beady eyes and pointed chin, Lester reminded Susan of the fat gray rats that swam in the Hudson River. Susan turned away from him, hoping he hadn't seen her, but it was too late.

"Why, Missy O'Neal, 'tis a pleasure to see you."

Susan cringed inside. She always had the feeling that Lester's Irish accent was fake. Dad had sworn Lester made it up to get the Irish people to vote for him. Nothing about the man seemed genuine.

"I trust your mother is well."

How could she be, Susan thought, *when she's worried sick about scraping up the monstrous rent you charge?* Lester was twice as impatient for his rent as the other landlords in Chelsea. Other landlords tried to be accommodating— they knew their tenants were poor, not dishonest, and they would wait six months, even eight months, before demanding their rent. But all Susan said was, "Mum's as well as you'd expect, Mr. Barrow."

"Good, good. Now I need to talk to you for a minute." He pulled Susan aside. "Thursday after next. 'Tis the end of the month. You know your mother's rent is due." His grip on Susan's arm tightened. "She's four months behind, lassie. I've been more than patient with her, knowing her circumstances. But I must have my money by the end of the month. 'Tis a business I'm operating, not a charity."

Susan tried to push down her rising panic. There was no way Mum could have all the money by then. Lester would put them out on the street; she knew he would. She'd seen him do it to the Laskys, the Polish family who'd lived in the basement flat. Susan stammered, trying to think of something to say to buy Mum more time, even a couple of weeks. Who knows what could happen in a couple of weeks?

"Oh, Mum can get the money, Mr. Barrow. I'm sure she can."

"I'm glad of that. I truly am. I have the highest regard for your mother, understand. The widow of a fine Democrat like your dad. That's why I felt obliged to help your mother get a job." Lester's voice was oily-smooth. "And why I've tried to look after your family since your dad's been gone."

Susan thought bitterly that Lester had done nothing of the sort. In fact, he had worried Mum to death about making the rent.

"But there's only so much a man in my position can do," Lester went on. He shook his head and clucked. "If your mum can't afford my building, 'tis time she thought of moving perhaps. Flats in Five Points go for five dollars a month, I hear."

Five Points was the worst slum in New York, as Lester well knew. This was a threat, and one Lester would make good on. Frantically Susan scoured her brain for a reply. Then she remembered the new boarder. "No, we can afford your building. We can now. Mum advertised for a boarder in the *Times*. A British woman answered—a Miss Rutherford—and she's arriving today. The rent will be caught up in no time, you'll see."

Lester's eyes narrowed. "A boarder?"

Suddenly Susan was afraid she'd said the wrong thing. What if Lester raised the rent? What if a boarder was against the rules? Her stomach churned as she waited for Lester's response.

All he did was grunt. "Tell your mother I may stop by after my meeting this evening. If it's not too late. I want to meet this boarder."

Lester released his hold on her, turned, and strutted out the door.

Susan put a hand to her cheek. She'd done nothing but make things worse. Now Lester was coming by tonight instead of next week!

Susan shuffled back in line. Instantly Helen was beside her. "What did Mr. Barrow say to you, Susie?" Her eyes were wide with apprehension.

"Nothing." Still shaken, Susan tried hard to hold her voice steady. "Just asking for the rent like he usually does." She couldn't let her little sister know how desperate their situation was.

By the time Susan reached the counter, she was in no mood to bargain with Mr. D'Attilio. She snatched the day-old bread he gave her for her nickel and whisked Helen out of the bakery.

The girls walked in silence the remaining block to their tenement building. Susan wondered how much longer they could stay in this familiar neighborhood. She'd lived in Chelsea all her life. What would it be like living in a place like Five Points?

Suddenly Susan felt tired. She wanted to go home and flop on her bed and sleep for a long time. But she couldn't. There was too much to do. She had to pick up Lucy at the Cochrans', where Lucy stayed while Mum was at work. Then she had to get ready for the boarder, which meant hauling water from the common sink in the hallway, peeling potatoes, and cutting up cabbage. There'd be no time for reading now.

"Susie!" Helen's voice cut into Susan's thoughts. They were in front of their own redbrick building.

"What is it?" Susan asked.

"Our window. I saw someone in there."

Susan looked up at their window on the fourth floor. There was nothing. "Helen, stop imagining things. You turn everything into a scene from a movie. I wish you would—" Then she stopped and stared.

A dark form had passed in front of their window.

Someone was in their flat!

CHAPTER 2

A FIGURE IN THE WINDOW

"Did you see it?" Helen's eyes were big as saucers.

Susan nodded.

"Do you think someone's broken in? The Jimmy Curley gang?"

"I don't know." Susan struggled to keep fear out of her voice. Why did Mum have to work late *tonight*? "Maybe our eyes are playing tricks on us. Mrs. Flynn put an idea in our heads, and now we're imagining things."

"*That's* not our imagination." Helen pointed to the shadowy figure in the window. There *was* someone in their flat, and Susan had the eerie feeling that person was looking directly at them. Fear knotted her stomach.

The wind, blowing cold off the Hudson River, whipped rain into Susan's face. She glanced around, hoping to see the precinct policeman leaning against the lamppost where he often stood to watch children playing stickball in the street. But he was nowhere in sight. In fact, the streets were empty of all but a few people hurrying along the sidewalks, huddled under raincoats or umbrellas. Rain was falling in sheets now, plastering Helen's hair to her head and soaking through her coat. She was shivering hard.

Just like Dad was when he came home from the docks the night he took sick. And he was dead from pneumonia within two weeks.

Susan had to get Helen inside. She shifted her gaze back to the window. Now she saw nothing there.

But Mrs. Flynn's warning rang in her ears. *Jimmy Curley. Fresh out of Sing Sing.* No, she wasn't going to risk it. They would just have to go to the Cochrans' and wait till Mum came home. Mum would know what to do.

"Come on, Helen," Susan said, and pulled her sister up the stoop and into the foyer. They hurried past the brass letterboxes and into the dark stairwell.

Up four flights they went, then to the landing, into the hallway, past the Dwyers' door, past the Thompsons', and here they were, standing outside the Cochrans' door. From the other side of the door they could hear the sounds of the Cochran kitchen: the clatter of pots, the drone of voices, a chair scraping across the bare linoleum floor.

We're safe now, Susan thought.

But somehow, now that they were at the Cochrans' door, the idea of a gang from Sing Sing robbing their flat seemed silly. Suddenly Susan was sure their fears would sound ridiculous to the Cochrans. Especially to Russell. He was one of Susan's best friends, but he dearly loved to tease.

"Helen," Susan whispered. "Let's not say anything about prowlers. If we're wrong, Russell will tease us to death. We'll just have a nice visit with the Cochrans until Mum gets home—"

Then came a loud thump from down the hall—behind their own door! Susan's heart leaped into her throat. Helen fell onto the Cochrans' door, knocking furiously. Susan was right behind her. They nearly tumbled inside when Mrs. Cochran opened the door.

"There's someone in our flat!" Helen cried. "A robber! From the Jimmy Curley Gang!"

"We heard something in our flat, is all," Susan said, trying to sound mature and reasonable in spite of her racing pulse.

"And we saw someone in the window!" Helen threw in.

"Ach, you girls are soaked." Mrs. Cochran was already stripping off their coats. Her voice was gentle and motherly.

"But the prowler!" Helen protested.

"'Tis only your boarder, dear," Mrs. Cochran said, patting Helen's shoulder. "She got here early and I let her in with the spare key."

Susan felt her face color. Why hadn't she thought of that? How silly they must seem! Out of the corner of her eye, Susan saw Russell perched on a chair by the stove, his face in a geography textbook, laughing. She resolved to smear him into the pavement in their next game of stickball. Then she pretended not to notice him. "Where's my sister, Mrs. Cochran? We ought to get home and start dinner for the boarder."

"Lucy? She's in our room for a nap. You girls toast in front of the stove while I get her."

Helen moved quickly to the warmth of the stove. Susan, though her fingers ached with cold, had no desire to get near enough to Russell to be teased. She seated herself at the far end of the table and let her thoughts drift to the boarder—this Miss Rutherford—who was at that very moment settling down in *their* flat.

How would it feel to have a stranger living with them in their cramped three-room flat? The boarder was to have Mum's room, and Mum would sleep in the closet off the kitchen. It was all cleaned out, the broom and mop set in a corner of the kitchen and the cleaning powder, mothballs, roach powder, and such set on top of the icebox or pushed into the crowded china cabinet. A little white cot for Mum had somehow been squeezed into the closet and her belongings stacked on the shelves behind a tacked-on curtain. Susan hated to think of Mum sleeping there while a stranger took over the room Mum and Dad had shared. But Mum always said you do what you have to and make the best of it, so Susan tried not to think about it too much.

She pictured Miss Rutherford in her mind: tall and thin, with a pinched face and sharp, demanding eyes, snapping out commands in her British accent. Susan dreaded the very idea of meeting her, yet she knew Mum was depending on her to make Miss Rutherford feel at home. Susan heaved a deep sigh.

Then Mrs. Cochran emerged from the bedroom carrying three-year-old Lucy, her blond head slumped on Mrs. Cochran's shoulder. Lucy was rubbing her eyes with her fist. "I wants my Susie," she said in her sleepy voice, and it warmed Susan's heart. Maybe it wasn't so bad being a big sister after all.

The girls left the Cochrans' and stepped out into the freezing hallway. Lucy instantly started sniffling and announced she was cold and hungry. "I want some butter bread," she whimpered.

The bread! Susan had left it on the Cochrans' table. Well, she wasn't about to go back after it. Not after the way Russell had laughed at her. "Isn't any bread, sweetie. You'll have to wait for supper."

Wait a minute. Wasn't that cooking meat Susan smelled? Drifting from their flat?

Helen was sniffing, too. "Something smells good. Like roast," she said. "Maybe the boarder's fixing roast for dinner. Our dinner." Her voice was bright.

"Maybe." Susan's mind was racing. It was definitely meat, roasting in *their* oven. Where on earth did the boarder get meat? Not in the empty O'Neal icebox, that was for sure. It had been months since Mum brought anything home from the butcher's.

"Come on, Susie." Both her sisters were eager to go in, but Susan hung back. A stranger at Mum's big black stove, cooking their dinner? It didn't seem right.

Yet she had to admit that without a boarder they would probably lose their home. So there was nothing to do but take Mum's advice—do what you have to and make the best of it.

Susan took a deep breath and pushed the door open.

❧

Warm air enveloped the girls as they stepped into their kitchen. It was almost stifling after the chilly hallway. Had Miss Rutherford completely emptied the coal box into the stove? What did she think they'd do for heat the rest of the week? Susan felt sick thinking of it, despite the delicious smell wafting from the oven. And there was a big pot bubbling on the stove.

But there was no sign of any boarder.

"There's no one here," said Helen.

"Doesn't appear to be," Susan said. She was already checking the other rooms—Mum's closet and the two bedrooms. She even opened her bedroom window and looked out on the fire escape. Nothing there but the gray street below, deserted in the pouring rain, and the street lamps' dim circles of light struggling to break through the gloom.

It was all beginning to be a little spooky.

Anxiety crept into Susan's stomach as she returned to the kitchen. "Nothing. No sign of a living soul."

"The table's even set for us," said Helen.

"It's magic," Lucy piped. "Do you think it's elves, Susie?"

Susan jumped as a voice from the hallway announced, "I used to *pretend* I was an elf. When I was little. Does that count?"

Across the threshold stepped a young woman wearing a linen suit trimmed with buttons, and a wide-brimmed hat wrapped in a cloud of pink chiffon. In one hand she held a dripping umbrella, in the other, a bundle tied with string. She was short and plump, pretty, with twinkling eyes. This was Miss Rutherford? Not at all what Susan had imagined.

"My name's Beatrice Alexis Victoria Rutherford," she said, shaking the umbrella. Droplets of water flew onto the blistered walls of the kitchen and the scuffed linoleum floor. "Too much of a mouthful for anyone but the queen, don't you think? You can call me Bea."

"That's not a name," giggled Lucy. "That's what gets on the flowers in Chelsea Park and stings you if you're not careful."

"Well, I don't sting. And I've never been to Chelsea Park, as I arrived in New York only today. Much earlier in the day than I had planned, I might add. May I come in?"

Susan wanted to say, *No, go home, back to England. I don't want you here.* But of course she couldn't, so she stepped aside for Bea to pass.

"Thank you, love." She plopped her bundle down on the table. "Since I arrived so early, I thought it was only fair that I pick up a few things for dinner—a nice leg of lamb, some carrots and onions. I had dinner nearly ready when I realized I'd forgotten the bread, so I popped down to the baker's on the corner. They were just closing, but I managed to talk the nice baker into giving me the last of his fresh bread. After all, I told him, he could only sell it for half price tomorrow. I must have been quite convincing, really. He ended up making me a present of two loaves."

Bea pulled off string and damp brown paper to reveal two round loaves. "This one's pumpernickel. The other's plain white. I like both. I hope you do, too."

Lucy nodded vigorously. "I likes butter on my bread."

"Butter you shall have, dearie. What's your name?"

"My name's Lucy. It's easy to say."

"That it is," laughed Bea. "Enough chatter, though. Lucy wants her bread. We'll eat straightaway."

"Shouldn't we wait for Mum?" Susan asked.

"There's plenty and more, love. Your mum would want you fed. I'm sure of it."

How can you be sure of it, Susan thought, *when you don't even know my mum?*

But Susan was too hungry to put up an argument. She bolted down the meat and vegetables, and even took seconds. Bea didn't eat; she sipped a cup of tea and chatted away while the girls gobbled seconds and thirds.

Bea was bright and cheery. Lucy and Helen were quickly taken with her, and even Susan couldn't help enjoying herself.

With her stomach full and the room so warm, Susan began to feel comfortably sleepy. Soon Lucy's head was nodding. "I say, let me get this girl into bed," Bea exclaimed.

"No!" Lucy's head popped up. A piece of potato clung to her hair. "I'm not sleepy!"

"Why, I didn't mean you, dearie. I was talking about myself. I've had a long day, and I'm quite tuckered. Would you sit in my lap and listen to a song while I rock? It would help me relax ever so much."

Lucy scrambled from her chair into Bea's lap. "My mummy sings to me, too. Will you sing 'My Bonnie'?"

"Don't know that one, love. I had in mind an old sea ditty my uncle used to sing to me. He was captain of a clipper ship, he was. Sailed the seven seas, had a wooden leg, the whole caboodle." With that she began to sing. Halfway through the second chorus, Lucy was asleep. Bea tiptoed into the bedroom and put her in bed. Then she insisted on fetching water and washing up the dishes herself while Susan and Helen got a start on their lessons.

"Can't very well let those boys show you up in class, now, can you?" she said with a wink.

Susan pulled out her English book and started conjugating verbs, but she couldn't keep her mind on *teach, taught, teaching.* All she could think about was Bea— Bea, who was elbow-deep in dishwater and humming away. Susan liked Bea, she did. She couldn't help it.

CHAPTER 3
A SECRET

Soon afterward, Mum came dragging through the door, a puddle of water in her wake. The alarm clock on top of the icebox read half past eight.

"It's raining cats and dogs," she said. She sounded weary. Water was dripping off Mum's hat into a pool on the floor, and she was shivering.

Bea scurried to take off Mum's wet things. "You look like you swam home, love," she said. "Why didn't you take the subway?"

"Pshaw," said Mum. "No reason to spend good money on the subway. I won't melt. You must be Miss Rutherford." She smiled and held out her hand in greeting. "I hope my girls had a nice dinner ready when you got here." Susan felt a stab of guilt. She hadn't done anything Mum had asked her to.

"Why, they gave me a lovely welcome," said Bea. "I just added the meat and a few carrots and onions to spice dinner up a bit. Sit down and try some. You've got jewels in those girls, love, that you do."

"I do indeed," said Mum. She smiled and kissed Susan and Helen on the head.

Bea took pains to get Mum warm and dry, then sat and ate with her. Bea told stories all the while, funny stories about her relatives back in England. She had them all laughing, even Mum, until tears ran from their eyes. Susan couldn't remember the last time she'd seen Mum laugh so hard; surely it was before Dad died.

Then right in the middle of Bea's story about her Welsh cousin who herded sheep, there was a knock at the door. Susan feared it was Lester Barrow, come even before she'd had a chance to warn Mum, but it was only a man bringing Bea's trunk from the depot. Then, of course, Susan had to tell Mum about Lester, which wiped the smile from Mum's face and brought back her tired, haggard expression.

"A plague take that Lester Barrow!" said Mum. "He *must* know I'm doing the best I can." She sighed. "Perhaps if I give him three dollars more on payday, he'll wait for the rest."

"That's half your week's pay, Mum!" Susan was thinking of the coal they'd be needing.

"Yes, but what else can I do?"

"Ask for a raise," Bea said. "I don't have the pleasure of acquaintance with your boss, but it sounds as if he's taking advantage of you, love."

To Susan's surprise, Mum agreed with Bea. "That he does. He pays us women half what he pays his male clerks." She sighed again. "I think you're right, Bea. I need to make more money, and that's the short of it. I just might ask for a raise."

Mum's words worried Susan. Discontent was dangerous down on the docks where Mum worked. Susan remembered Dad telling them about a couple of longshoremen he worked with who'd disappeared. They were colored men, Dad said, and they were assigned the worst job on the docks—unloading the dark recesses of the ship's hold. These men, it seemed, made the mistake of complaining to the union about their work conditions. The next day they didn't show up for work, though they had never missed a day in ten years. No one ever saw them again. Dad figured they had ended up at the bottom of the river.

"Mum, I'm not sure you should do that," Susan worried. "Remember those men Dad worked with who disappeared . . ."

"Ah, and you think the same thing might happen to me." Mum reached across the table and patted Susan's hand. "Don't think so, lamb. Mr. Riley's hard to work for, it's true, but he's a Tammany man. He'd never do such things to a woman—it would be against Tammany code. No, the least I can do is ask, and the worst he can do is say no.

"It's paying Lester Barrow four months' back rent I'm worried about now." She sighed. "I suppose I'll have to stay up and wait to see if he comes by, though I would dearly love to go straight to bed."

Mum yawned. "Run on to bed, Helen and Susie. I'll be in soon to tuck you in."

Helen obeyed, but Susan hesitated. Whether from worrying or from the excitement of the day's events, she felt wide-awake. "May I stay up with you and wait for Lester Barrow?"

Before Mum could answer, Bea asked if Susan would like to help her unpack and get settled.

Mum accepted for her. "Susie's a marvelous helper, Bea." Mum patted Susan's hand. "You go on, lamb. I'll sit here and rock awhile." She was already settling into the rocking chair.

Susan nodded. If it would make Mum happy to keep Bea happy, Susan would do her best to oblige. She followed Bea into "her" room, empty now except for the bed, lumpy with age, the nightstand, and the dresser. The bare look of Mum's room sent a pang shooting through Susan, but she knew this was Bea's room now, and there was no use wishing it wasn't. Besides, she couldn't help being curious about that huge trunk of Bea's. What on earth could she have in there?

Susan eagerly watched Bea unlock the trunk and open the lid. An awed "ooh" escaped her lips as Bea began unpacking beautifully embroidered, lacy linens and nightgowns of finer fabric than Mum's Sunday blouse.

"Would you put these away for me, love?" Bea handed Susan the folded linens.

Susan fingered the smooth, silky fabric. "What are they for?"

"To sleep on," Bea said, smiling. "I know they're rather fancy, but they were my mother's, and I couldn't bear to leave them behind."

Susan tried to imagine lying between such sheets. "Your mother slept on these?"

"When she was very young. Her family was wealthy once, but the fortune's gone now." Bea reached into the trunk and took out a stack of handkerchiefs.

"Tell me about your schoolwork, Susan."

Susan told Bea about her English class. "We have to write an essay on a theme from the novel the teacher chose for us. Most of the kids grumbled about it, but I *like* writing—and reading, too—so it suits me fine." She sighed. "I just don't know when I'm going to have time to read the book. It's really long, and . . ." She hesitated, thinking how Bea's arrival had kept her from starting the novel. "Well, I have to help Mum out a lot around here."

Bea's voice held understanding. "Not much time to do the things you enjoy, is there?"

Susan shook her head. "But I don't mind helping, most of the time. Mum's got enough to worry about as it is." Susan stroked the linens once more, then slid them into a drawer in the dresser.

"I'm sure your mum appreciates your help, Susan, as I do." Bea handed Susan a couple of nightgowns to put away. "I love reading, too. It was painful leaving most of my books behind—like parting with family. I nearly cried. What book do you have to read for your English class?"

"It's called *Middlemarch*. My teacher said she thought I would particularly enjoy it. I've never heard of the author, though. George Eliot, or something like that."

Bea's face lit up. "George Eliot is one of my favorite authors. And I love *Middlemarch*. It's one of the few books I chose to bring. I've read it many times, and each time I find something I've never noticed before. There are a couple of passages I'd like to show you. It's here in the trunk somewhere, I know. We'll find it."

Bea was so lively and seemed so genuinely interested in her that Susan soon found herself chatting easily. While they talked, Bea continued to hand Susan more belongings from her trunk to put away. There were skirts and blouses, jackets, a cape, and beautiful underclothes trimmed with lace—camisoles, corsets, stockings. And there were several hats. Mum had only one, the wide-brimmed straw hat Dad had given her for Easter two years ago. Mum always hung it on a hook on the wall, like she did with her dresses—the three or four that she had. But there weren't enough hooks on Mum's walls for the hats and clothes Bea had told Susan to pile on the bed.

"Oh dear," Bea said, as she apparently came to the

same conclusion. "What was I thinking, bringing all these things? I suppose they'll have to go back in the trunk once we're done."

Bea's matter-of-fact attitude toward her beautiful clothes perplexed Susan. Mum fussed so over the few dresses she had—hanging them neatly, ironing and mending—and she taught Helen and Susan to do the same. They all had to make clothes last as long as possible.

Bea's manner changed, however, as she lifted out of the trunk a rectangular package tied in brown paper. She loosened the strings gently, then lifted away the paper to reveal a framed photograph. Bea looked at the photograph intently for a moment, then ran the fingers of one hand along the frame's edge.

Curious, Susan couldn't keep from leaning over Bea's shoulder. Bea glanced up, then smiled at Susan and handed her the photograph. "Careful, love, this means quite a lot to me."

Susan had never seen such a lovely frame. It was heavy, made of rich, polished wood edged with gold. The photograph was of Bea and some other women, arm in arm, in a city scene with statues of lions in the background. "Where was the photograph taken?" Susan asked.

"Trafalgar Square. In London. It's like your Times Square here." The women, Bea said, were some of her good friends back in England. "This one"—she pointed out an older lady—"was like a mother to me. She and her daughter, here"—she pointed to a very pretty younger woman with blond hair—"helped me find direction in my life when I needed it." She took the frame from Susan and carefully placed it on the nightstand.

Susan wondered what sort of direction the women had given Bea. Had that direction led her here, to New York City, and to Chelsea? After all, it was a little strange that Bea, with all her beautiful things, should choose to rent a room in this old building. It seemed she could afford to board in a nicer place, a brownstone maybe, or one of the new apartment houses uptown. Curiosity itched at Susan, but she knew it would be rude to ask.

Besides, Bea was furiously rummaging through the remaining contents of the trunk—mostly books and bundles of papers—pulling them out and stacking them on the floor. "I remembered what I did with that book," she said. "It was the first thing I packed, because I didn't want to forget it. So it's got to be at the very bottom of the trunk. Ah, here it is." She smiled as if she'd just found an old friend. "*Middlemarch,* by George Eliot."

Susan sat on the bed beside Bea to look at the book.

"You'd never guess by the name, but George Eliot was a woman." Bea sounded as pleased as if George Eliot had been her sister. "She was one of the most noted authors of her day. She feared her writing would never be taken seriously if it were known she was a woman, so she used an alias, a pen name. I like her because her female characters are women who know their own minds. There's nothing weak or wishy-washy about them. They rely on themselves to get what they want."

"You mean the *heroine* gets to kill the dragons and catch the bank robbers?"

Bea laughed. "Something like that. I've marked my favorite passages. Flip through and see what you think while I decide what to do with the rest of this rubbish in my trunk."

Susan took the book and eagerly began to turn the pages. She was curious to see what passages Bea had under-lined. Susan spotted an interesting part at the bottom of the page that reminded her of her own feelings this after-noon—something about being *hemmed in by a life which seemed nothing but a walled-in maze of small paths that led nowhere*. She flipped to the next page to finish it.

When she did, a folded piece of paper—it looked like a letter—fell from between the pages onto the floor. As Susan reached to pick up the letter, her eye fell on the words *must be kept secret for now*.

Bea looked up from her packing and spotted the letter lying on the floor. "I wondered what I had done with that letter," Bea said. She whisked it up and stashed it in the drawer of the nightstand. Then she said brightly, "What do you think of the book?"

❧

Lying in bed that night, Susan thought about Bea's letter and the words that she had seen: *must be kept secret for now.* A strange sensation tingled Susan's spine, and she wasn't sure if it was fear or excitement. In a way, it was glamorous to think of having not an ordinary boarder, but a boarder with a *secret.*

What *was* Bea's secret? Susan's imagination spun out countless possibilities. The one that intrigued her most sprang from the newspaper headline this afternoon. Bea's betrothed was a spy for England. He was to be sent deep into enemy territory, perhaps to Berlin itself, on a mission that *must be kept secret for now.* He feared for Bea's safety if his mission should be discovered, so he sent her to America until the war was over. Susan's heart beat faster with the adventure of it all, and she couldn't go to sleep for a very long time.

Chapter 4
Bluffing

Bea's secret was still on Susan's mind when she woke up in the morning, and she couldn't resist telling Helen about it.

Helen immediately got stars in her eyes. "No, no, no, I'm sure you're wrong, Susie. I'll bet it's a *love affair* that Bea's keeping secret. Bea's probably engaged to a wealthy Englishman whose family doesn't like her. Maybe they think she's too poor, so he has to wait to marry her until after he inherits his money. I saw the same thing in one of Mary Pickford's movies."

Susan raised an eyebrow. "I suppose a secret engagement would be more likely than a spy mission, though I think I'd rather it be the spy mission. That's much more exciting."

The girls continued to whisper about Bea's secret for the next few days. Susan even told Russell about it, though she swore him to secrecy. He, too, liked the idea of a spy mission, but he convinced Susan that Helen's guess was probably closer to the truth. "Nothing as exciting as spying would ever happen on 26th Street," he said. Susan reluctantly agreed.

As a week passed, however, and then another, and cold, gray September drew to a close, it wasn't so much Bea's secret that fascinated Susan as it was Bea herself.

Bea seemed different from the other women Susan knew. Susan couldn't really explain how; Bea was just . . . *different.*

Bea had a talent for making everyday things special. She was a wonderful cook. She bought fresh vegetables every day from the pushcart vendors and prepared them in strange and wonderful ways. Cabbage and potatoes, the staples of the O'Neal diet before Bea arrived, were given new life under Bea's hand. They became cabbage rolls, potatoes au gratin, and shepherd's pie. She also came home with meat several times a week and sometimes pastries from D'Attilio's. "You girls," she said, "all need fattening up, and your mum, too. You're skinny as rails." She fixed them British dishes, like sweetmeats and mince pies, and when Lucy turned up her nose at trying them, Bea pretended to be the witch in "Hansel and Gretel," fattening Lucy for the oven. Lucy loved it and always ended up cleaning her plate.

But it was more than that. Susan herself felt different around Bea. Maybe it was the way Bea asked so many questions—not nosy questions, but wondering questions—the same kinds of questions that went around in Susan's head. Sometimes Susan would catch Bea staring off into space. Susan would ask her what was wrong, and Bea would say, "I was just thinking, love." Then she would tell Susan what she was thinking about.

That's what Susan liked best about Bea: Bea *talked* to Susan. Not in the way most grown-ups talked to children; instead Susan always felt that Bea truly valued her opinion. When Bea was reading—and she read a lot, like Susan did— she would often stop and read a passage aloud to Susan and ask Susan what she thought about it. Then Bea would carefully consider whatever Susan said. Sometimes she would ask questions about Susan's comment that made Susan think in a new way about the passage. And some- times Susan would ask questions that Bea claimed made *her* think in a new way. Susan began to think of reading as more than simply an enjoyable pastime; talking to Bea turned reading into an *adventure.*

In fact, talking to Bea made even the drudgery of Susan's chores seem almost fun. When Susan had to wash dishes or scrub the floor, Bea worked right alongside her, and they talked as they worked. It wasn't long before Susan found herself telling Bea things that she hadn't even told Mum, like her dream of going to college. To Susan's surprise, Bea encouraged her to pursue it. "If something is truly important to you," Bea said, "you can usually discover a way to achieve it."

Susan noticed that Bea was very skillful at discovering

ways to do what *she* wanted. She found a job at the Nabisco factory the very first day she went out looking. Bea said she and her boss got along famously, and they must have, for Bea didn't seem to work nearly as much as the other Nabisco employees Susan knew. Bea's hours were unusual, too. She was always changing shifts, sometimes working during the day and sometimes in the evenings. Susan chalked it all up to Bea's powers of persuasion. She could talk people into anything and make them think it was their idea all along. Just the way she'd talked Mr. D'Attilio into giving away his fresh bread.

Yes, Susan told herself, Bea was different. And her presence had made a difference in the family. Mum seemed happier; she smiled more. Mum and Bea stayed up late at night talking. It was comforting to hear the murmur of their voices as Susan drifted off to sleep every night. It reminded her of the days when Dad was alive and she had fallen asleep each night to the sound of Mum's and Dad's voices in the room beside her.

❧

October came to Chelsea warm and golden, one sunny day following another. It was almost as if Bea had brought Indian summer with her. The sun shone every day from a clear blue sky, and across the river Susan could see wooded hills glowing gold and red with autumn colors.

The weather was so fine, and Mum seemed so much happier, Susan nearly forgot about Lester Barrow and the overdue rent. Until one day when she came home from school and found Mum already home from work. Mum wasn't feeling good, Bea said, and she was resting in bed.

Instantly Susan thought of Dad, coming home sick one day, dead two weeks later. Panic rose in Susan's throat. "Mum's sick? I have to see her."

Bea, concern on her face, glanced at the closed door of the closet where Mum slept. At that moment the closet door opened and Mum appeared. The waning sun filtering through the single window framed Mum's face in shadows.

"Thank you, Bea, for giving me time to rest." Her voice trembled, and when she stepped out of the shadows, her face became that of someone Susan didn't know: an old woman, pale and hollow-eyed. Mum looked as if she had aged years since she left for work that morning. What had happened to her?

Mum slumped down at the table, and Bea put a cup of tea in front of her.

Susan watched Mum mechanically lift the cup to her mouth. Lucy was chattering away, but Mum scarcely took note of her. She seemed to be far away from the dingy kitchen. Something was horribly wrong. Susan glanced at Helen, searching for a clue, but Helen's baffled expression said she didn't know any more than Susan did. Even Bea was subdued, talking quietly to Lucy.

Finally Mum sighed, and the sigh seemed to bring her back to them. "I don't know what I'm going to do. Lester Barrow came to see me at work today. He can't be helping me forever, he says." Her voice dropped to a whisper. "I'm afraid our time is running out."

Susan was horrified.

"What happens if you can't pay him soon?" asked Helen.

"I'm afraid we'll be moving to Five Points, little one. There's nothing more I can do."

Bea set down the knife she'd been using to butter bread for Lucy. "Let's think about this a minute. What Lester Barrow really wants is his money. If you move, he loses all the rent you owe him, as well as a tenant. If he believes there's the smallest chance of getting paid, he's not likely to throw you out. Am I right?"

"You're making sense. But he knows I can't pay, or I'd have done so already."

"Ah, there's a secret to dealing with men like him."

Mum looked up from the table.

Bea spoke slowly. "You must appear calm and confident when you talk to him, like this." She paused, Susan guessed, to let the effect of her voice sink in. "Never show despair. Even if you're frightened to death of him, don't let him know it." Then her tone became urgent. "I tell you, Rose, despair is our worst enemy. Men like Lester will use it against us time and again. They've always used it against us. They know it makes us roll over and give up, rather than fight."

Susan was confused. Who was Bea talking about? What did she mean by *us*?

Mum's brow furrowed. "I don't know, Bea. I can't see Lester being fooled by a change in my attitude."

"I'm not thinking he'll be fooled, simply unsettled. He'll see you can't be frightened by his bullying, and—" Bea's eyes darted to Helen and Susan, both listening intently, then back to Mum. "We'll talk about it later, Rose, all right?"

Mum nodded, but Susan thought she still looked doubtful.

Anxiety lay heavy in Susan's belly. She wanted to believe Bea was right, but she was almost afraid for Mum to try what Bea suggested. It seemed like playing with fire to try to trick Lester, even if Bea said it wasn't really a trick. What would happen to Mum when Lester realized she had been stringing him along? Susan didn't want to think about it.

She asked to be excused and headed to the fire escape outside her window. The fire escape was Susan's retreat, a place she could be alone to think or to watch what was going on in the street below. Russell's fire escape was two windows over from Susan's, and sometimes they met out there to talk, away from the listening ears of parents and brothers and sisters.

As soon as Susan stuck her head out her window, she saw Russell on his fire escape, reading. Her first reaction was disappointment; she'd wanted to be alone. Then she decided it might be a relief to talk to him.

"Hi, Sue," he said as she climbed out. "I'm just now getting started on my book for the essay assignment. *Great Expectations.* I can't seem to get interested in it."

Susan smiled. Russell said that about every book he had to read for school. "Russell, the essay's due in three weeks."

"I know, but I haven't had time to read, what with working two jobs. Did I tell you about my new job at the barbershop over by Penn Central Station?"

Susan rolled her eyes. "Only two or three times." In fact, Russell had been bragging ever since he got the job about all the money he was making selling morning news-papers *and* shining shoes at the barbershop after school and on Saturdays.

Russell went on about his job as if he hadn't heard Susan. "My boss, Mr. Delaney, takes a cut of all our tips—he says it's his right since it's him who hires us out to the barbers—but I still average around two bits a day. I give half of that to Ma, but the rest I add to my newspaper money and save. You'll see, it won't be long now before I can buy a bicycle for my delivery service." Russell had been saving for over a year to start his own delivery service when he finished grammar school.

"That's grand, Russell, grand," said Susan. "I would think you'd be a favorite with your boss, making him that much money every day."

"Oh, yeah."

An idea was taking shape in Susan's head, a tiny grain of an idea that grew with every word Russell said about his job. It was a way she could help Mum get caught up on the rent. She believed it would work, if only Russell would help her. "I'm glad your boss likes you, Russell. That means you can put in a word for me, so I can get a job with him, too. Mum's behind on the rent, and I'd really like to help her out."

Russell looked at her as if she were a thick-skulled dunce. "There's no way Delaney's going to give a girl that job, and you know it."

"But he may give it to me," Susan said, "if I pretend to be a boy."

Russell stared hard at her, but now there was a light in his eyes. "This I've got to hear." He closed his book with a bang. "You're telling me that you want to go to Delaney disguised as a boy?"

"Sure. I'll wear one of your caps and an old pair of knickers. He'll never know the difference."

Russell screwed his mouth to one side and studied Susan. "You've got the hair already." A few months ago, Susan had talked Mum into giving her one of the new bobs all the girls were getting. "It just might work." A smile spread across his face. "I like it. Old Delaney's always working us to death, taking tips that should be ours. What a lark to see someone get the best of him. And a girl at that." He chuckled. "When do you want to go?"

"Better sooner than later," said Susan. "You talk to him tomorrow, then I'll go down the day after."

⚡

"Sammy MacGowan, huh?" Mr. Delaney peered over his spectacles at Susan.

Susan's heart thumped against her ribs so hard she was sure Delaney could hear it. Russell's clothes itched, and his cap on her head was too big. It kept falling over one eye. Susan concentrated as hard as she could on Bea's words to Mum about showing confidence even when you didn't feel it. Then she answered boldly, "Yes, sir."

Delaney's curly eyebrows knit together. He scrutinized her as if she were a plump turkey hanging in Paddy's Market.

Did he suspect something? Could he tell she was a girl? Susan's palms sweated.

He scowled.

Susan was sure he saw through her disguise. Maybe he would throw her out into the alley. Maybe he was on the verge of calling a policeman. She had the urge to run, but she held it at bay.

"You're Irish, aren't you?"

Relief washed over her. Is that all he was worried about? Susan was used to dealing with people's prejudices about the Irish. "Yes, sir, I'm Irish, but I work hard."

"You're small."

"I'm quick, sir."

"You think so? We'll see about that. You've got one day to prove yourself, boy. Any tips you make today I keep." He was scribbling on a scrap of paper. "Here's the barber you'll be working for. Do you know the address?"

Susan nodded, but she swallowed hard. The address was on 36th Street, on the northern border of Chelsea. It was one of the toughest neighborhoods in the city. It was called Hell's Kitchen.

CHAPTER 5
INSIDE HELL'S KITCHEN

 fter the first few days of work at the barbershop, Susan's apprehension left her. Hell's Kitchen was not that much different from Chelsea—dirtier, perhaps, and the residents poorer and more desperate. Yet her customers were generally decent, honest people.

Although shining shoes was hard work, Susan enjoyed proving that she could do it, and do it as well as the boys—even better. She made it a point to arrive at the barbershop early enough every day to get organized before the shop got busy. She would set up her stand with shine rags and brushes on one side and her polish bottle, paste wax, and suede brushes on the other—everything always organized perfectly so that her hands could fly from brush to polish to rags without her ever having to take her eyes from her work. She also learned that if she popped the shine rag across the shoe, making a sound like a firecracker, the customer thought she was really hustling and would give a bigger tip.

After a couple of weeks, Mr. Delaney was actually praising the job she was doing. Susan figured that those large tips had a lot to do with his attitude. Some Saturdays she made as much as fifty cents.

Susan saved her money and kept it hidden in the bottom drawer of her bureau. She was proud of how much she was saving, and she wished she could tell Mum and Bea what she was doing. She had decided from the start, though, to keep her work at the barbershop a secret. She knew Mum wouldn't approve of her using deception to get the job, so she led Mum and Bea to believe she was working on her essay every afternoon at the library. She hadn't really lied to them, but she hadn't been totally honest either, and she felt guilty about it. She told herself, though, that she was doing it for the good of the family. When Lester Barrow threatened Mum again, Susan would be ready with money to help her. Then she would tell Mum the whole story, and if Mum wanted her to quit the job after that, she would.

Though it was ten blocks to the barbershop, Susan refused to spend her money on carfare. She made a game of seeing how many different routes she could take to work. Sometimes she crossed to Eleventh Avenue and walked by the Borden train terminal to watch the refrigerator cars full of milk and ice cream being unloaded.

Sometimes she would go one block farther to 12th so she could walk past the Chelsea Piers where Dad used to work. The piers were connected along the street front by a continuous bulkhead that had huge arched windows and a gabled roof at the entrance to every pier. Susan thought the piers were the fanciest buildings in Chelsea. If she went by way of 12th past the piers, she was careful to avoid Pier 67 between 28th and 29th. On that block was the office of Hudson River Shipping, where Mum worked.

During her third week at the barbershop, Susan was walking up Ninth Avenue past the post office when she thought she saw Bea on the crowded post office steps talking to a fashionably dressed older woman. Susan ducked behind a pillar of the elevated train overpass and looked again. It *was* Bea. Susan had walked right past her, and Bea hadn't recognized her in Russell's clothes.

What was Bea doing up here when she was supposed to be at work? The Nabisco factory was way down on 14th Street. And who was that society lady she was talking to? The woman looked like she belonged in Gramercy Park instead of on Chelsea's crowded streets—she even had a little pug dog dressed in a sweater at her heels. What possible business could Bea have with such a wealthy-looking woman?

While Susan was puzzling on this, another strange thing happened. Lester Barrow came out of the post office and greeted Bea as if he knew her. Susan couldn't hear what they said, but Lester and Bea were both nodding and laughing, and Lester shook hands with the society lady. He even reached down and petted the little dog. They talked for a few minutes, then walked down the steps to the street together. Finally, Lester tipped his hat to the ladies, walked up the avenue, and disappeared into the crowd of pedestrians.

Susan stood in the gloom of the underpass, scarcely able to believe what she had just seen. If she hadn't known better, she would have thought Lester and Bea were old friends. Susan had never seen Lester act so gracious to anyone. She could see why he would be courteous to the rich lady—but to Bea? Bea was a nobody, a woman who boarded with tenants in his own building. Why would Lester be so gracious to *her*? And, Susan wondered, why would Bea act so friendly to *him,* knowing the way he had threatened Mum?

Susan puzzled on it the rest of the way to the barbershop, but she couldn't figure it out. And she certainly couldn't ask Bea about it, not without risking giving away her own secret. The incident nagged at Susan all afternoon. A voice in her head kept whispering that perhaps she didn't really know Bea as well as she thought she did. *After all,* said the voice, *Bea's been with you scarcely more than a month. How can you know a person in such a short time?* Susan closed her ears to the voice's murmuring. She *did* know Bea. Bea was practically part of the family, the big sister Susan had never had, and Susan was sure there was a reasonable explanation for Bea's behavior.

Yet Susan was even more perplexed by Bea the following evening. Mum came home upset because her friend at work, Kathleen, had been fired. Mum said that Mr. Riley had accused Kathleen of not working hard enough, but Kathleen claimed Mr. Riley had found out she'd marched in a suffrage parade and had ordered her to condemn the suffrage movement. When she refused, he fired her.

By the time Mum finished her story, Bea was red in the face, and her eyes had a fire in them that Susan had never seen. "What did you do about it?" Bea demanded of Mum.

"What did I do?" Mum looked confounded. "There was nothing I *could* do. Riley never listens to any of the women around the office."

"Why didn't you stick up for Kathleen? If every woman in the office had threatened to quit, your boss wouldn't have dared sack her. His business would have come to a standstill."

Mum chuckled bitterly. "His business would have stood still for half an hour at most. That's how long it would take him to replace us, and he knows it. If any of us had said a word, he would have fired us in a snap. And we need our jobs."

"So you stood by while Kathleen lost hers—because she believed in a cause." Susan had never heard Bea speak so harshly.

"A cause doesn't pay the bills. Kathleen's stand was very noble. And very foolish."

"You think suffrage is foolish, Mum?" Susan asked.

Susan was shocked by the intensity of Mum's reply. "Why are you twisting my words, Susan? I'm trying to say that there are reasons why some people can't stand up for causes, even if they believe in them!" With that Mum jumped up from the table. "I'm going for a walk," she said. She slammed the door behind her.

Mum had not come home by the time Susan went to bed. Later, Susan was awakened by Bea and Mum arguing in the kitchen. Susan strained to listen as their words came through the darkness.

"What you're doing for us is splendid," Bea was saying, "but you could do more."

Bea was talking about "us" again. *Who in the name of heaven,* Susan wondered, *is "us"?*

Mum said something that Susan couldn't make out.

Susan heard Bea again. "You can't be paralyzed by fear. That's what they want. I know how you feel—"

"No, you don't!" said Mum. "You come from—"

The rest was drowned out by the rattle of a passing train.

Then Susan heard Bea slam her bedroom door and

mumble to herself in the bedroom. Susan knew she shouldn't, but she put her ear to the wall to try to hear what Bea was saying. All she could make out were a few words. Something about a war and beating them at their own game.

Anxiety began to creep up Susan's spine. What did Bea want Mum to do?

Suddenly Bea's secret came crashing back into Susan's brain. Maybe it wasn't a romance Bea was hiding after all. Maybe it *was* something to do with the war. Susan's heart pounded. Thoughts of spying and secret missions again raced through her head. *Dangerous* secret missions. Was Bea trying to involve Mum in something dangerous?

No, Susan told herself fiercely, *Bea wouldn't do that.* Maybe she didn't know *everything* about Bea, but she knew her well enough to feel certain that Bea wouldn't intentionally put Mum in harm's way. Besides, the idea that Bea might be a spy—why, that was just Susan's imagination running wild. Russell was right, Susan told herself. That sort of thing happened in books and faraway places, not in humdrum Chelsea.

Susan tried her best to put it all out of her mind and go back to sleep, but every time she closed her eyes, some noise—the elevated train rumbling by, an argument in the flat downstairs, a cat wailing from the alley—would jar her. Finally she felt herself drifting off.

The next thing she knew, she jerked awake. She'd been dreaming of Dad, and his face was as vivid before her eyes as if he had tucked her into bed that night. The anguish of missing Dad came to her more keenly than it had in months. Her throat ached; a massive weight pressed on her chest.

Susan slipped from the warmth of the covers and crawled off the bed, careful not to wake her sisters. She crept into the kitchen, slipped out into the hallway, and ran two flights up to the roof.

Far below, the backyard light illuminated the gray wash pole and the clotheslines spreading like silvery spiderwebs across the yard. Incandescent lights from shopwindows, left on all night, glowed red, and the blinking lights from boats moved sleepily up and down the river. The baritone of a ship's horn drifted across the water.

Susan knew no lonelier sound in the world, and it pierced her with such a feeling of emptiness, she began to cry. Huge, rolling sobs poured from deep inside her. She covered her face.

Then she felt a hand on her back. It was Bea. Bea took off her robe and put it around Susan's shoulders. "A bit chilly to be out in your nightgown. What's wrong, love?"

Susan's voice came out raspy. "I . . . I dreamed about Dad, and it made me wish for him so much."

"I know, love." Bea pulled Susan close to her. "What was he like?"

What was he like? Why, he was the best father a girl ever had. But how could Susan make Bea understand? "Well, he was big—he towered over Mum—but gentle. He didn't have to be tough. His voice was enough to make you jump. And he was redheaded like me. Some people said he had an Irishman's temper, but he never lost it—hardly ever—around us. He laughed all the time—" Then she couldn't go on. The lump in her throat was too big.

At first Bea didn't speak. Then she said, "I should've liked such a father. I never knew my own dad. My grandfather was the man in my life. An important member of Parliament he was." This she spoke with a regal, put-on voice. "But he was so stern, I was afraid to go near him."

"How old were you, Bea, when your grandfather died?" Susan asked softly.

Bea stared out across the river. "He's not dead. We had rather a nasty disagreement a few years ago and haven't spoken since. I've no other family to speak of."

Bea sounded so dismal, Susan longed to comfort her, but she didn't know how.

"You're fortunate," Bea said, "to have fond memories of your dad. When I was little, I had to imagine mine. Oh, did I come up with some doozies. My favorite was the one where my dad and I had tea at Buckingham Palace. The queen herself poured, as I recall. Tell me your favorite memory."

"It's hard to choose just one," said Susan. "But I really liked going with Dad to Slocum's for egg creams." Susan told Bea how much fun she and Helen had had going with Dad to the candy store on 30th Street and sipping the rich, chocolaty drinks that were called egg creams. They'd each have two glasses, even Dad.

"Do you ever go there anymore, you and Helen?"

Susan shrugged. "Nah. Egg creams are a nickel each. Besides, half the fun was being there with Dad."

Bea nodded. "I know. That was the best thing about tea at the palace, too. At least your dad, though, was real."

"Yeah, but it hurts when I think of him, so I try not to."

"It hurts because you loved him so much. The best you can do with pain, love, is to make something good come out of it. Remember the kind of man your dad was, and try your best to live in a way that would make him proud."

Bea's words turned a light on in Susan's brain. For the first time she saw her memories of Dad as something to be treasured and enjoyed rather than avoided as too painful. She felt the heaviness in her chest begin to lift a little. As it did, a warm feeling toward Bea replaced the heaviness. Bea understood Susan in a way that no one else ever had. Susan thought she'd never had so special a friendship.

For a while both Susan and Bea were silent. Finally Susan asked, "Do you still care for your grandfather, Bea?"

"I suppose I do. Since my mother died, he's all I have."

"Do you think he still cares for you?"

"I . . . don't know. I imagine he does. In his own way. Why do you ask?"

"I was just thinking that if you and your grandfather cared for each other . . . well, you're still family, aren't you? No matter what's passed between you. Couldn't you just put it behind you?"

Bea didn't reply. The moonlight was too dim to read her face. Susan rushed on. "Maybe if you spoke to him first . . . if you wrote him or something." She hesitated, not knowing what to say next.

Susan was relieved when Bea spoke. "I don't think it would do any good to write him. My grandfather's a stubborn man."

"Wouldn't it be worth a try? Maybe he's forgotten what you disagreed about."

"Oh, no," Bea said fiercely, "he hasn't forgotten. I should have to buckle under to his way of thinking to make peace with him. And there's no way I'll do that." Susan could feel Bea's whole body shaking.

Her reaction startled Susan. "I didn't mean to upset you, Bea. I was just wondering . . . well, I was trying to help . . ."

"I know you were, love." Bea's voice now was calm and warm. "What were you wondering?"

"I was wondering what you disagreed about."

Bea stiffened just a little. "It's hard to explain, Susan." She paused. "Let's simply say he wants me to be something that I can't be." Then she put her arm around Susan. "I say, it's getting colder. We'd better get you back to bed."

CHAPTER 6
THE SUFFRAGE PROBLEM

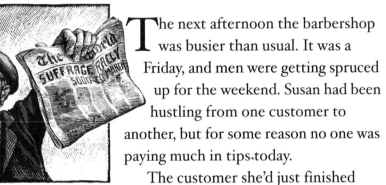

The next afternoon the barbershop was busier than usual. It was a Friday, and men were getting spruced up for the weekend. Susan had been hustling from one customer to another, but for some reason no one was paying much in tips today.

The customer she'd just finished with was a Tammany man, she was sure. Tammany men were always well dressed. This fellow had been wearing a stylish waistcoat, as well as leather boots that he wanted spit-shined. Susan took extra care, even using special polish that cost her a dime a bottle. When he reached in his pocket to get a coin for her tip, she saw he had a large, expensive watch chain, and she expected a tip of at least a nickel. But when she opened her hand to look at the coin, she saw he had given her only a penny, not even enough to cover the cost of the special polish she'd used! And half of that would go to Delaney! She couldn't believe she'd wasted so much time on the man. All she could do was try to hustle even more to make up her loss.

Still fuming over the man's stinginess, Susan scurried toward a group of men in lounge suits talking in the back of the shop.

"Shine, anyone?" she asked.

"Aye, lad, right here, and be quick with you," a man barked from the back of the group.

The voice was familiar. Susan struggled to place it.

"Hurry up, lad—I'm a busy man. Move aside, Bigelow, so the boy can get through." He shoved at the fat man in front of him. When Bigelow moved, Susan saw too late the face of her customer. It was Lester Barrow!

Susan knelt and set to work on Lester's oxfords. She pulled the shine cloth furiously back and forth while her heart pounded. What if Lester recognized her? What would he do to a girl who made a fool of him by posing as his shoe-shine boy?

Susan yanked her cap down almost over her eyes, but she needn't have worried about it, for Lester was too involved in his conversation with the other men to notice her. She soon realized he wasn't paying her any more attention than he was the flies on the wall, and she relaxed a little. She pricked up her ears, however, when she heard Bigelow mention "the suffrage problem."

"Those biddies are going to kill our system," Bigelow was saying. "They're already soapboxing on what they're

going to do when they get the vote, how they ain't going
to tolerate no corruption in their government. They're
going to clean up city hall, they say. Why, that's us! *We're*
city hall, and we've got to do something before they sweep
us right out of our livelihood!"

"Bigelow's right," said a tall man with a hook nose.
"We were so sure that the men of New York would never
give women the vote, we've allowed these frantic
females—I won't call 'em ladies—to pick up more and
more support every year. There are states west of the
Mississippi, gentlemen, where women are already voting!
It's high time we admitted it could happen here—to our
ruin. We must act now, *decisively*, to crush their movement
before it's too late!"

A murmur of agreement rippled through the group.

Then Lester spoke. "Ah, my friends, is that all the faith
you have in your district leader? Haven't I steered the
party in the right direction these last ten years? Have I
ever once failed to move with the speed of a striking adder
when the situation called for action?"

How fitting, Susan thought, *that Lester would compare
himself to a snake.* He was as cold-blooded as a reptile, that
was for sure.

Lester's shoes were as shiny as they were going to get,
but Susan continued to shine, hoping that Lester would
say more about his plans to defeat the suffragists.

And what snaky plans they turned out to be! Lester

had already arranged, he said, for "a little ruckus" at the rally the suffragists had scheduled for Saturday. "As you know," he chuckled, "the police force, the mayor, and half the judges in town are in Tammany's hip pocket. Those biddies will think twice before they stir up discontent again in my town!"

All the men laughed heartily, apparently convinced that the "suffrage problem" would soon be solved. Their laughter was scornful, and it made Susan angry. Lester and his friends were no different from those boys who threw tomatoes at the suffragist in Chelsea. Why should women wanting to vote make people act so hateful?

Susan couldn't get their laughter out of her head, and she was still thinking about it when she finished up at the barbershop and started home. She trudged along the noisy, fitful streets, tuning out the din of traffic and ignoring the press of pedestrians on the sidewalk. It was the same as always this time of day—people hurrying, pushing, a swirl of coats and hats and skirts, faces strained, impatient, horns honking, trolley bells ringing, traffic cops whistling traffic through intersections. Always the same.

On 30th Street, the newsboy stood at his usual post in front of the police station, hawking the evening edition of the *Times.* He was crying out headlines, same as usual, but this headline caught Susan's attention. It was about tomorrow's suffrage rally!

"Read all about it! An army of women to march on Saturday five thousand strong!"

"How much for a paper?" Susan asked the boy. He was red-faced, and younger than Susan. He looked like he was Helen's age. His stack of newspapers was almost as big as he was.

"A penny, miss."

Susan dug in her pocket for a penny and eagerly scanned the front page for the article on the rally. There, she found it: a photograph at the bottom of the page showing some of the suffragists who would speak at the rally. On one side was an article and on the other side, an editorial.

Over five thousand women from every state in the Union were expected to show up for the parade down Fifth Avenue to Central Park, the article said. There would be bands, floats, and an automobile procession. Men would also be joining the parade; a drum and fife corps would head their division.

Then she began to read the editorial, and she grew angrier with every line. The editorial ridiculed the suffragists, calling them home wreckers, dangerous, petty, and other words Susan didn't know the meaning of. But what really made Susan mad was what the editorial said about women in general:

> *That the female mind is inferior to the male mind need not be assumed: that there is something about it essentially different, and that this difference is of a kind and degree*

that votes for women would constitute a political danger, is, or ought to be, plain to everybody.

Despite the big words, Susan got the message loud and clear. The writer was claiming that females were not as smart as males. Well, she knew one thing for sure—Russell's mind was not superior to hers. She always made better marks than he did at school.

It was Lester Barrow's attitude all over again: if women vote, terrible things will happen. The editorial writer, Lester, Mum's boss Mr. Riley—they all seemed afraid of suffrage. Why?

Susan thought back to the bold suffragist she had heard speaking in Chelsea. She couldn't remember much of what the suffragist had said, but it didn't seem like anything people should be afraid of.

Now Susan's curiosity was really aroused. She looked again at the picture of the featured speaker for the rally. Alice Paul, the caption said. She looked like an ordinary woman to Susan. What could this woman have to say that stirred everybody up?

There was one way to find out, and Susan made up her mind right there on the curb that she would do it. She would ask Mr. Delaney for the day off and go to the suffrage rally herself. And she would ask Russell and Helen to go with her.

At dinner, Susan discovered that the rally was not the only unusual thing happening on Saturday. Mum told the girls she was getting the day off work tomorrow to visit Aunt Blanche. Aunt Blanche was Dad's elderly aunt who lived on a farm on Long Island. Aunt Blanche was ailing, Mum said, and had asked her to come. "I'll be leaving on the 6 A.M. for Long Island, and I'm not sure what time I'll be returning."

Susan looked up in surprise. Mum was going to spend fifty cents on train fare to visit a distant relative she didn't even like? *Oh, well,* she thought, *at least I won't have to explain to Mum where Helen and I will be tomorrow.*

"You'll need to watch Lucy for me, Susan," Mum said. "Bea has to work."

"But I can't!" Susan said. If she had to watch Lucy, she couldn't go to the rally. "I've made plans for the day."

"Then you'll have to change them. This is not a request." Mum's face was beginning to flush. "We've all pitched in and done extra so you could be free to work on your essay in the afternoons. Now when I ask you to care for your sister so that I can have a day to do something I need to do, you balk at it?" Her eyes flashed.

Susan had lost her appetite for the stewed cabbage on her plate. She asked to be excused, but she wouldn't look at Mum.

She was careful not to stomp on her way back to her room. No use giving Mum more reason to be mad at her.

No, Mum would be angry enough when she found out Susan had gone off and left Lucy with Russell's mother for the day.

Because nothing was going to stop Susan from going to that suffrage rally tomorrow. Nothing.

చ

Mum and Bea were both gone when the girls got up Saturday morning. There was a note to Susan on the kitchen table. It was from Mum, apologizing for snapping at her and marked with two long lines of Xs—Mum's kisses. The note made Susan feel guilty about disobeying Mum to go to the rally, but not guilty enough to change her mind.

Now Susan, Russell, and Helen were on their way, the trolley lurching and bumping along Fifth Avenue. The suffrage parade was to begin at one o'clock, and the rally would follow in Central Park. Russell and Helen seemed to be enjoying the ride, despite its bumpiness. Susan tried to lean back and relax as well, but she was too excited, and there was too much to see. Though she had lived in the city all her life, she had never been this far uptown.

Uptown was a different world from Chelsea. Instead of run-down brick tenements, uptown streets were lined with quiet, dignified brownstones behind wrought-iron fences and with elegant stores and apartment buildings where uniformed doormen waited. Pierce-Arrows and Packards were parked on the curbs, not the milk-wagon nags and Model T's seen on Chelsea's curbs. There were fancy restaurants and office buildings with ornate facades and arched windows.

Even the uptown people were different. No one hurried here. Pedestrians sauntered along the street, lolling in front of houses or store windows. Men in suits with narrow trousers strolled arm in arm with women in feathered hats and fur-trimmed jackets. Mothers pushed infants in prams along the sidewalk.

As the trolley crossed 50th Street, Susan's heart beat faster. Cars draped with yellow banners were already in line for the parade. The line must have stretched the entire nine blocks up to Central Park.

Once off the trolley, Susan, Russell, and Helen hurried to find a spot on the sidewalk amid the crowd that was already gathering to watch the parade. Mounted policemen patrolled the avenue trying to keep the crowd in order. By the time the parade began, a solid wall of spectators hung behind the ropes stretched across the sidewalk. Susan wondered whether they all supported suffrage or were only here to gawk at "the dangerous home wreckers" that the *Times* had reported would be marching.

Soon the bands struck up and the marchers came, hundreds of women in yellow sashes, striding confidently through the sea of spectators, their yellow banners floating in the wind. Susan thought it was a thrilling sight.

And the men were marching, too, just as the newspaper said they would. There were countless bands and floats, an endless procession of automobiles, drums beating, trumpets tooting, horns honking. Susan's pulse quickened with every beat of the drums.

Susan tried to look at every face, all the marchers, as they went by, to see if she could figure out what it was about them that made people so angry. But there were too many marchers to see them all, and they went by too fast. Besides, they looked so ordinary. They looked like all the other men and women Susan knew, and the people she saw on the streets of the city every day.

Later, at the rally, Susan felt her heart thrill again when Alice Paul began to speak. The rest of the crowd melted away for Susan. All she saw was the platform where Alice Paul stood; all she heard were the words Alice Paul spoke in her strong, vibrant voice.

"Our movement isn't just about the rights of women," Miss Paul said. "It's about the rights of individuals—all of us here—to participate in the freedoms of our country, a country founded on the principles of fairness and justice, but a country which denies fairness and justice to those of its citizens who happen to be female.

"Yes, my friends, our country tells us that we as females are not entitled to be treated fairly. You and you and you"—here she pointed to women in the audience—

"are not entitled to be treated as your brother is, or as your father is, or as your husband is.

"Our movement is about the rights of individuals," she continued, her voice lowered. "All of us here. Every man and woman, every boy and girl, must travel through life individually, and, individually, face life's challenges. There will be difficult times in every girl's life, every woman's life, when she *must* be prepared to depend on her own resources—whatever strength, whatever comfort or guidance she finds within herself. She *must* rely on herself.

"It is a cruel thing indeed to rob an individual of her right to rely on herself. And that is exactly what those who oppose votes for women are doing."

She went on to talk about the way women for more than sixty years had worked quietly and ineffectively, asking for consideration as full citizens of this country. "The time of quietness is past," she said. "We intend now to sound our voices loudly and clearly to the lawmakers of the land. They will know the strength of our anger. It is high time that we cease to politely ask for the vote. From this day forward, my friends, we will demand it!"

Susan's heart swelled. She had never heard a woman speak like this. Susan was so caught up in Miss Paul's speech that it took her a few minutes to notice what was happening in the crowd. Then she saw that spectators up near the platform were getting rowdy; someone began shouting at Miss Paul, and a few more people joined in.

At first Miss Paul ignored them, but soon the shouting drowned out her voice. Another suffragist on the platform, the woman who had earlier introduced Miss Paul, stepped to the podium and tried to outshout the hecklers, asking them to have some respect for Miss Paul. Someone hurled a half-eaten ice cream cone and hit the suffragist in the face. The crowd laughed. Then someone threw a tomato, which set off a barrage of fruit, rotten vegetables, even eggs being thrown at the suffragists. Suddenly, Susan realized Lester's "ruckus" had begun.

The rowdiness quickly spread through the crowd. People started pushing at anyone who was wearing a yellow sash. Banners were ripped off the stage and torn from women's hands.

To Susan's surprise, the police didn't make a move to stop the rowdiness. In fact, they seemed to spur the crowd on. Susan heard a policeman yell to one of the suffragists that she deserved a lot more than an egg in the face. It wasn't long before the front of the crowd had become a brawl. The police got out their clubs, but Susan thought they seemed more eager to club the suffragists than anybody else.

Farther back, where Susan, Russell, and Helen were standing, the crowd was getting agitated, and some people were moving forward toward the brawl. "We've got to get out of here," Russell said to Susan, "before this whole place breaks into a riot."

The pandemonium spread. The crowd surged forward, and the three children were swept along with it. People were jostling and pushing, packed so close that Susan could scarcely breathe. Russell had seized Susan's sleeve and was screaming at her to grab hold of Helen a few feet in front of them. But the press of people was closing in on her, and Susan couldn't move. Two men beside Helen started slugging each other, and one of them fell against Helen. Susan watched, horrified, as Helen stumbled, then went down under the feet of the crowd.

CHAPTER 7
CAUGHT IN THE RIOT

Helen!" Susan screamed, but her voice dissolved into the human sea. Helen was nowhere to be seen. Terror seized Susan. She shook off Russell's grasp and pressed forward, squeezing between the people in front of her, thankful for once that she was small. Her eyes swung right and left, searching for Helen amid the swirling confusion.

And finally, there was Helen, struggling to stand up in the tide of people. Susan screamed at her again, and this time Helen heard and turned toward Susan, her face etched with fear.

"Give me your hand!" Susan called. Helen pushed a thin arm up through the tangle of legs, and Susan pressed forward, closer, grabbed Helen's hand, pulled; and there was Russell, too, pulling, and finally Helen was in Susan's arms. Tears were streaming down their faces. She was

holding Helen so tightly she could feel her sister's warmth
against her.

"Come on!" Russell yelled, beckoning toward a break
in the crowd. The children pushed toward the gap and
forced their way out of the press of people. Fresh air
rushed into Susan's lungs. She could breathe again. She
checked Helen over, every inch of her. As soon as Susan
was sure Helen was all right, the three hurried away
toward the trolley.

Susan looked back only once. The police had finally
begun to break up the riot. Some people were being
arrested and carried to paddy wagons waiting nearby.
Good! The hecklers and rowdies would spend the night
in jail. No less than they deserved.

Susan dropped a dime into the trolley's glass jar, fare
for her and Helen, and watched the conductor crank the
coin down the transparent chute into the till below. Then
she slid into a straw-colored seat next to the window,
where she could see the troublemakers being hauled away.
The trolley jumped to a start just as the paddy wagons
were rumbling by.

But it wasn't the rowdies being carted off to jail at all!
It was the suffragists, still wearing their yellow sashes!
Susan couldn't believe it.

By the time the trolley lurched to a stop at the corner of Eighth Avenue and 26th, the rooflines of Chelsea were stretched tight against a darkening sky. Stores and cars had begun turning on their lights, and the Nabisco factory was blowing its whistle announcing the 6:00 shift change.

At home, the girls found an empty flat. Bea was not home yet from the factory. Susan got Lucy from the Cochrans', fed her some cornmeal mush, and put her to bed. An hour passed, and Bea still hadn't come. Anxiety flickered in Susan's stomach. Where was Bea? Susan reheated the mush for herself and Helen. Helen ate just a few bites before she fell asleep at the table, and Susan could only pick at her own food. She settled Helen in the rocker, then sat at the table and watched the hands of the clock creep to half past eight.

Why didn't Bea come home?

Now anxiety was gnawing at Susan in earnest. Whispered stories hovered in the back of her mind—stories about workers injured at the factories. The story of the horrible fire at the Triangle Shirtwaist Factory only a few years before, when more than a hundred workers had died, trapped in the blazing building.

What if something equally awful had happened to Bea?

At nine o'clock Susan couldn't stand it any longer. She roused Helen and then went to Russell's and asked if he would go to the Nabisco factory and check on Bea.

Time inched past. The girls huddled together in Mum's rocker and watched the clock move to 9:30, 9:45, 10:00.

"Where *is* she, Susie?" Helen kept asking. Susan just shook her head. If she spoke, she might betray the fear rumbling in her belly. *What a time,* Susan thought, *to be here alone without Mum.*

Finally, finally, came the sound of a key turning in the door. Maybe it would be Mum; maybe it would be Bea. Susan didn't know who she wanted to see more. The knob turned. The door opened, and Bea appeared. Relief washed over Susan, but concern instantly replaced it.

Something was wrong with Bea. She was moving slowly, with the greatest of effort, like old Mrs. Hannish with her rheumatism.

"Bea! What's wrong?" Helen exclaimed.

Bea claimed to be fine. "I'm sorry to be so late, girls. I hope you didn't worry. I'm just a bit tired and sore from a long day at work. I'm going straight to bed." Yet the spark was missing from her voice. She hobbled across the kitchen, not looking to right or left, not speaking, not even noticing Mum's absence.

Bea's bedroom door clicked shut.

For a minute Susan and Helen stared at each other, then at Bea's closed door. "Something's not right," Susan whispered. "I'll try to talk to her."

Susan tapped on Bea's door.

"Who is it?"

"Me, Susan."

Susan thought she heard Bea sigh. "Come in."

Susan opened the door. Bea was standing, facing her. "What is it, Susan?" Bea's voice sounded strained, and Susan noticed with a twinge that she hadn't called Susan "love."

"Mum's not home yet. We're getting worried."

"I shouldn't worry about her. Perhaps your aunt needed her to stay a bit longer. Your mum knows I'm here to take care of you girls."

"I guess you're right," Susan said hesitantly. It seemed, though, like Mum would have gotten word to them if she was staying over. Susan stared absently at Bea's Trafalgar Square photograph on the nightstand. She doubted Aunt Blanche had a telephone, but Mum could telephone from town, couldn't she, and leave a message for them at Rubenstein's Drugstore on the corner?

Bea had moved toward the nightstand, and now she reached down and angled the photograph away from Susan's view. It struck Susan as a rather strange thing to do at the moment. "Was there something else?" Bea asked.

"Yes! Are *you* all right, Bea? You're limping."

"A bit of a sprain I got at work. That's why I was late. Don't mention it to anyone, hear me, love? It's a trifle, really." She eased herself onto the bed. "If you don't mind, Susan, I'm terribly tired. Would you shut the door on your way out?"

Susan was stung. Bea had always welcomed her company. Now she was brushing Susan off, as if she was a pesky child. As Susan closed the door, she thought she heard Bea moan. *Something* was wrong.

Reluctantly, Susan went back to the kitchen. She found Helen asleep in the rocker. She led her to bed and tucked her in beside Lucy, but Susan was too anxious to sleep. Bea seemed to be in pain, and Susan couldn't do anything to help her. She kept hoping that Mum might still show up this evening. Then Mum could do something about Bea. Susan went back into the kitchen to wait. She sat at the table and tried to read, but her eyes kept swimming. She couldn't concentrate.

The fire in the stove had died, and the room was growing cold. The flat seemed so empty without Mum . . .

Susan jerked awake to a knocking at the door.

Mum! She must have forgotten her key!

Susan rushed to the door and flung it open, but it wasn't Mum. It was Russell.

"Oh, it's you," Susan said. Swallowing her disappointment, she turned from the door and slumped in the rocker. "I thought you might be Mum. Bea came home already, Russell, but thanks for going to check on her."

Russell stepped into the kitchen and grasped Susan's arm. "You're not going to believe what I found out."

"What are you talking about?"

"I went to the Nabisco factory. I found the second-shift foreman. Had a nice long talk with him."

"That's grand," said Susan wearily. "I'm glad you enjoyed meeting the foreman."

"I did. He was a capital fellow. He had some interesting information."

"I'm not in the mood for this, Russell. I'm worried."

"You ought to be."

Suddenly Russell had Susan's full attention. "Why?"

"Your boarder's been lying to you," he said. "No Beatrice Rutherford has ever worked at the Nabisco factory."

CHAPTER 8

LESTER'S VISIT

Susan sprang out of bed at the first hint of dawn, hoping that Mum would be home. But the door to Mum's closet stood open, the bed not slept in. In the kitchen, gray light filtered through the curtains. Mum was not there. Mum had not come home.

Disappointment rippled through Susan, disappointment tinged with anxiety. Why didn't Mum try to get in touch with them? She was bound to know they'd be worried about her. It didn't seem like Mum at all.

Bea was again her cheery self. She made hot cocoa and promised the girls an outing in the park after breakfast. Susan could have sworn, though, she saw Bea wince as she reached into the cabinet for cups.

Helen gulped down her cocoa and asked for seconds; Lucy buzzed about the outing all through breakfast. But Susan only sipped at her cocoa and nibbled at her toasted cornbread. She didn't have much of an appetite. She was worried about Mum, and Russell's words from last night lay like stones in her belly.

Why had Bea lied to them about her job?

The only thing Susan could figure was that Bea was embarrassed about the job she did have. Maybe she was working as a maid somewhere, perhaps for that rich woman with the pug dog. Someone like Bea, Susan guessed, might feel ashamed of doing domestic work. It hurt Susan, though, to think that Bea felt she couldn't be honest with her. After all, Susan told her nearly everything. She'd have thought their friendship was special enough for Bea to do the same—to have trusted Susan with the truth, if no one else.

"You've barely touched your breakfast, love." Bea's voice broke into Susan's thoughts. "Aren't you feeling well?" She felt Susan's forehead.

"It's my stomach," Susan said, and she told herself it wasn't really a lie. Her stomach did hurt, though not in the way Bea was thinking. "I don't think I'll go to the park."

Bea insisted on dosing Susan with castor oil and putting her to bed. She set a glass of water beside Susan's bed and tucked the covers around her. "Try to sleep, love. You were up late last night."

Susan wondered if Bea was feeling guilty for making the girls worry last night. She had an urge to tell Bea that she knew about her job, but something in Bea's eyes—was it sadness or pain?—kept Susan from doing so. What harm would it do, she thought, to let Bea have her secret?

Susan watched Bea walk quietly from the room, then listened to her and the girls in the kitchen getting ready to go out. Soon the kitchen door slammed. Susan knew she was alone.

From her bed, Susan stared out at the slice of sky she could see through her open window. Even though her view was marred by the fire escape, she could tell it was a beautiful morning. The smell of the ocean drifted in on a west-bound breeze. The same breeze whipped the smoke from the Nabisco factory into a soft, blue sky.

Susan usually felt as bright as the weather on a day like this, but today she felt tired and listless. She hadn't slept well last night. Visions of the violence at the rally had plagued her dreams, and she found herself wondering if it was more than a coincidence that Bea had come home injured. *Could Bea have been at the rally?* she asked herself. But she quickly dismissed the thought. She couldn't imagine why Bea would try to hide going to the rally. *Bea* had no Tammany boss like Mr. Riley breathing down her neck, threatening her to stay away from suffrage.

Susan must have dozed off, because she awoke with a start to the sound of a knock on the front door.

Mum!

It had to be Mum, for who would come calling on a Sunday morning? Susan leaped out of bed, flew to the kitchen, and flung open the door. Then her throat constricted. At her door stood Lester Barrow.

Her mouth went dry. Lester here to demand his money, and both Mum and Bea gone—what on earth was she going to do?

"Missy O'Neal. Good morning to ye." Lester tipped his hat and grinned in a way that made Susan shudder. He was wearing a gray, double-breasted serge suit, high-collared shirt, and silk tie. Susan figured he must have stopped by on his way home from church. "Did not see your family at Mass this morning. Your mother's not ill, I hope."

Susan's tongue was as heavy as lead in her mouth. She didn't know whether to invite Lester in or try to get rid of him. Finally, she heard herself stammer something about Mum visiting relatives for the weekend.

"And did she leave the rent with you, lass?" Lester was frowning.

Susan felt weak in the knees. She knew Mum was no closer to having all that money than when Lester had come to her office a while back and demanded it. Somehow Mum had managed to put him off then, but Susan had a feeling that Lester would not take kindly to being put off again.

Susan thought of her barbershop money, hidden safely

away for a moment like this. But the moment had come too soon. Her stash had grown so slowly, with Delaney taking half her tips, that Lester would probably laugh if she offered him the little she had.

Still, Susan had to do something. She couldn't just stand here forever like a statue. Susan repeated to herself what Bea had told Mum about using confidence to deal with men like Lester. Then she swallowed once, twice, invited Lester in, and offered him a cup of tea. All the while she was struggling to keep her hands from shaking and giving away her terror.

Susan shoveled a few lumps of coal into the stove and lit it. As she slid the kettle onto the burner, she said, "You understand, Mr. Barrow, Mum *has* the money, everything she owes you for the last few months." She reached into the china cabinet for two of their best china teacups. "The problem is, I don't know where it is. She left in such a hurry, I guess she forgot to tell me."

Lester looked puzzled. "But it's only for this month's rent I'm here, lassie. Your boarder, Miss Rutherford, paid all the rest quite some time ago."

Susan nearly dropped Lester's cup in his lap. *Bea had paid their back rent? Where had Bea gotten that kind of money?*

Praying her eyes didn't betray her shock, she forced a confident smile. "Oh, yes, I forgot she said she was going to do that. Care for sugar, Mr. Barrow?" A confident person, Susan was sure, would offer sugar to a guest, even if the guest was Lester Barrow. Luckily there was a teaspoonful left at the bottom of the sugar bin.

Lester accepted the sugar and stirred it into his tea. "You didn't tell me, Missie O'Neal, that your boarder was a cousin of your father's, and so highly connected at that—her grandfather in the British Parliament and all. It was kind of her, wasn't it, to come all this way to assist your poor widowed mother? If you'd only told me who she was, that day in the bakery, why, I wouldn't have been worrying a bit about getting my money."

Bea? Her father's cousin? That was ridiculous, Susan thought.

For a long moment Susan's mind was blank. Finally she managed to say something that she hoped sounded reasonable. "I . . . I didn't think about it, I guess. I was so excited, you know, about her coming, about meeting Dad's cousin." A nervous laugh escaped her lips, and instantly she scolded herself. She'd be in a fine position, wouldn't she, if Lester figured out she was bluffing . . .

But he didn't seem to notice. He finished his tea and wiped his mouth. Then he pushed himself back from the table. "I must be going, lassie. I've still the fifth floor to collect from, not to mention my buildings on 25th. Tell your mother there's no hurry on the rent. I know now she's good for it. She and your *boarder.*" He closed one eyelid in what Susan supposed was a wink.

Like a lizard blinking at a fly, Susan thought, *before it snatches up the fly for its dinner.* She shivered. "I'll tell her you were here, Mr. Barrow."

"Aye, you do that. I'll be back next week sometime. Perhaps when your charming cousin is here. Good day."

The door closed with a thud that echoed through the empty rooms. Susan stood still, listening, hardly able to believe that Lester was gone. She kept thinking that he might come bursting back through the door, chuckling in the same nasty way that he had in the barbershop, and tell her that it had all been a joke, that he was throwing them out on the street and taking Susan to jail for lying to him.

At last Susan was convinced he wasn't coming back. She collapsed in Mum's rocking chair and tried to straighten out her tangled thoughts.

Foremost in her mind was the fact that the overdue rent was all paid, that worry wiped away by Bea's generosity. Susan's heart swelled with affection for Bea, yet she wondered *why* Bea did it, and *how.* Susan supposed that Bea simply wanted to help out the family. Mum would . have objected to accepting charity, of course, but Susan guessed that Bea hadn't told Mum till after the rent had been paid.

The "how" posed more of a problem. Did Bea have that much money to just give away? Maybe Bea's family was more well-to-do than she'd led Susan to believe. But

if that was true, it presented the biggest puzzle of all—
namely, what in the world was Bea doing in Chelsea?

A chill ran down Susan's spine as the answer unfolded
inside her head: something that *must be kept secret for now.*

Susan gave a small, strangled cry. Bea's letter! She had
forgotten all about it.

In her mind's eye, Susan again saw Bea whisking the
letter off the floor and stashing it in the nightstand drawer.
As Susan recalled the incident, it occurred to her that
Bea had seemed awfully eager to get that letter out of
Susan's sight.

On an impulse, Susan got up and walked back to Bea's
room. She stood in the doorway, tempted to go in and
peek in the drawer, just to see if the letter was still there.

It was wrong to snoop, she knew, but she couldn't
forget that she'd caught Bea in one lie already. *If she's lying
about why she came to Chelsea,* Susan thought, *maybe we
should know about it.*

Susan thought of the conversation she'd overheard
between Mum and Bea, and Bea muttering about a war.
Had Susan been wrong at the time to ignore her fears
for Mum's safety?

Susan stared at the nightstand, struggling with her
conscience over whether to look for the letter. That was
when she noticed Bea's framed photograph was gone.
Susan's eyes swept the room, the nightstand, the dresser.
The photograph had disappeared.

At that moment, Susan heard a faint peal of laughter from the street below. She glanced out the open window and saw Bea and the girls returning from the park. Lucy was skipping down the sidewalk, holding fast to the string of a balloon. Bea and Helen were right behind, holding hands. Helen was nibbling on an ice cream cone; Bea had a newspaper tucked under one arm and a shopping bag in her free hand.

Now it was too late to look for the letter. Susan tried to swallow her fears about the secrets it might hold and went to meet Bea and her sisters at the door.

"You seem to be feeling better," Bea said, smiling. "And here we made a special trip to the pushcart vendors for all this food—"

"Bea said you needed a treat," Helen interrupted, "so I took her over to Tenth Avenue." Tenth Avenue was in the Jewish section of Chelsea. Since the Jewish Sabbath was Saturday, the pushcart vendors were out in force on Sunday.

"Bea got oranges, Susie!" Lucy said. She had chocolate ice cream smeared all over her mouth. "And see the pretty balloon she bought me?" She beamed. Lucy had never had a balloon, though she begged for one every time they went to the park.

Helen held out a small bag to Susan. "We brought you some candy, Susie. Horehound. Bea said it would help your stomach."

"We didn't suppose you would feel like ice cream," Bea added.

Susan thanked Bea and forced a smile. That missing photograph was nagging at her. Yesterday Bea had made a point of turning it away from Susan's view, and today it was gone. A small thing, maybe, but peculiar. And all these peculiar things about Bea were beginning to trouble Susan quite a lot.

Susan started unloading the shopping bag. There were oranges and bananas, a tin of cookies—Bea called them "biscuits"—four big pickles wrapped in paper, a slab of cheese—

Then Susan's eye fell on the newspaper Bea had placed on the table. *SUFFRAGISTS JAILED!* the headline shouted. Susan quickly scanned the article, her thoughts pulled back to yesterday's riot. According to the newspaper, the suffragists were being blamed for the violence, and the mayor had sworn to make examples of the women who were arrested. He promised that they would receive heavy fines and jail sentences. Susan shook her head. With Tammany Hall against them, how could the suffragists hope to succeed in New York City?

"You'll come, too, won't you, Susie?"

Susan pried her thoughts from the suffragists and looked down into Lucy's hopeful face. "Come where, sweetie?"

"Our picnic on the roof. Bea says we'll have cheese sandwiches and oranges."

"Yeah, sure, I'll come." Outings to the park and picnics on the roof—Susan wondered whether Bea was trying to keep them so busy they wouldn't have time to worry about Mum. It was only a stray thought, but it planted itself in Susan's head, and it stayed there the rest of the day.

CHAPTER 9
A TELEGRAM AND A LETTER

Mum still wasn't home by Sunday evening, and Susan's uneasiness turned to fear. Tomorrow would be Monday—a workday. If Mum didn't show up at the office tomorrow, she'd be fired. Something had happened, Susan was sure, something that was keeping Mum away.

Susan tried to voice her concern to Bea, but Bea insisted there was nothing to worry about. "Perhaps your mother made arrangements with Mr. Riley in case she had to stay longer."

Susan knew there was no such thing as "arrangements" for workers in Chelsea. If you displeased your boss, you lost your job, and everyone understood that's how it was. Everyone except Bea, it seemed.

Susan was too worried now to be satisfied with Bea's guesses about what *might* have happened. She wanted to know something for sure. "Can't you send a telegram to

Aunt Blanche? I just want to know that Mum is safe."

Bea touched Susan's arm. "You have *my* assurance, love. Isn't that enough?"

Susan fixed her eyes on a crack in the linoleum. She couldn't look at Bea because she knew her answer was no. Bea's assurances were no longer enough. Susan's heart beat faster as she realized what that meant. She couldn't rely on Bea anymore. She would have to take action herself to find Mum. First thing tomorrow she would wire Aunt Blanche.

❧

After dropping Helen off at school, Susan went to the Western Union office on 30th Street and plunked down a quarter from her barbershop money to send the telegram. All morning she hung around 30th Street waiting for an answer. She wandered over to the docks and watched the longshoremen unloading ships, but after a while, that made her heart ache for Dad. Which, in turn, made her worry more about Mum.

By three o'clock, she still had no answer, and she decided she'd better go on to the barbershop. The hours at the barbershop dragged by, and when six o'clock arrived, Susan stowed her shoe-shine kit and fairly bolted for the door. The long walk back to the Western Union office seemed endless. The sun cast long shadows of buildings

across the sidewalk in front of her. Hundreds of faces and
figures hurried past her, but Susan didn't see them. All she
thought about was her telegram and the reply that would
surely be waiting for her.

But there was no reply.

Her chest tight with disappointment, Susan rushed
out into the alley and nearly tripped over a scrawny dog
nosing in a garbage can. She had counted so much on that
telegram. Now her mind was a blur. She didn't know what
to do next.

Then it struck her that maybe she'd gotten no telegram
because Mum was already home!

She raced to 26th Street and the familiar red tenement.
Somehow she knew that Mum would be there. Mum
would be at the big black stove in the kitchen, humming
to herself as she fixed her girls their dinner.

Susan burst through the kitchen door, her lips already
forming words of welcome, but her hopes sank when it
was Bea she saw chopping cabbage on top of the washtub
cover. Mum was not home.

Bea was smiling. "I've got good news for you, love. I got
a telegram today."

Susan's pulse quickened. Could Aunt Blanche's telegram
somehow have been delivered to their flat while Susan was
at work?

"You needn't worry anymore about your mum," said
Bea. "She wired from Long Island. She's enjoying her rest

so much, she decided to stay on for a few more days."

Susan's first reaction was relief. *Mum was safe.* But as Bea's statement sank in, Susan's heart twisted: Mum, staying out of work simply to enjoy herself? It would never happen. Bea couldn't be telling the truth.

Susan opened her mouth to say so, then shut it quickly as she noticed Helen, sitting cross-legged on the floor with Lucy. Helen was wearing the most troubled expression Susan had ever seen on her face. And she was beckoning Susan toward the bedroom.

Once alone in their bedroom, Helen, in a frightened whisper, told Susan of the telegram's arrival only a few minutes before Susan got home. "I saw Bea's face when she opened it, Susie. The way she looked, it wasn't good news she was reading. She wouldn't let me see it when I asked to read it. There was bad news in the telegram— I know it."

"What are you saying?" A lump of fear was gathering in Susan's stomach. She knew very well what Helen was getting at.

Helen's voice sounded small. "I'm afraid something bad has happened to Mum, and Bea doesn't want us to know. Susie, I'm scared."

Susan pulled her sister close to her chest. She could feel Helen's heart pounding. "Don't be, sweetie. We don't know anything yet. We've got to get hold of that telegram and read it. That's all."

Helen pulled away and stared up at Susan. "How? Bea's got it in the pocket of her apron. We'll never be able to get it from her."

"If something is truly important, there's usually a way to get it." Bea's words sprang from Susan's mouth as naturally as if they had been her own. Susan's chest tightened painfully as she realized how Bea had become such a part of her. "Just give me a minute to think," she said to Helen. She paced over to the window and stared out at the shops across the street. From here she could almost read the labels on the cereal boxes stacked in the front window of Mr. Haggerty's grocery store. Then her mind jumped to the way Lucy always poured too much milk on her cereal. And then, Susan had an idea.

She knew exactly how they would get the telegram from Bea.

❧

At dinner that night, Susan ate slowly, waiting for her cue from Helen. Helen was chattering about the Girl Scout organizational meeting at the Hudson Guild that Mum had promised to take her to tonight. Helen was hinting for Bea to take her, but Bea was only half listening. Her attention seemed focused on the wall calendar next to the icebox. Susan glanced at Bea's plate; she'd barely touched her food. Bea was preoccupied with something, that was for sure. Susan hoped the telegram would tell them *with what.*

Finally Helen plunked down her empty cup on the table. "I'm still thirsty." She licked milky foam from her upper lip.

Susan stood up. "I'll get the milk. I want more, too."

Susan filled Helen's cup to the brim and handed it to her, but the cup slipped from Susan's hand and clattered to the floor, splattering milk everywhere. Then Susan knocked over the milk bottle. A white river flowed out and cascaded into Bea's lap. Smaller streams ran across the table and dripped over the side onto Lucy and Helen.

Bea leaped up, an astonished look on her face. She was soaked. A dark stain was spreading down her blouse, her apron, her skirt. Milk dribbled off her clothes onto the floor.

"Susie, you made a mess," said Lucy, eyeing first Bea, then her own flooded plate. Bea was holding her sopping skirt out from her body.

"Yeah," said Helen. "You managed to soak everything and everyone, except yourself." If Susan didn't know better, she would have thought Helen was really mad.

Susan hurried to help Bea take off her apron. "You better change, Bea, before you get chilled. I'll clean up out here." She began fetching rags from the ragbag under the dry sink.

"Come on, Lucy," said Helen. "You and I will have to

change, too." Helen marched Lucy to the bedroom, throwing an angry glance at Susan over her shoulder. Helen *would* make a wonderful actress, Susan decided.

Bea looked hesitantly at the sea of milk on the table and the floor. "I suppose I should get into something dry, but I'll be back to help straightaway."

As soon as Bea started down the hall, Susan stuck her hand in the apron pocket to snatch the telegram. Suddenly she heard Bea's voice. "Susan?"

Susan jerked her hand from the pocket. "Yes?" Had Bea seen her?

Bea was standing at the entrance to the kitchen. For a moment she was quiet. Then she said, "Don't feel bad, love. It wasn't your fault." With that, she disappeared into her room.

Susan felt a rush of guilt. She hated deceiving Bea. Then she hardened herself. Bea had brought it on herself, hadn't she, by deceiving them first.

Quickly Susan plunged her hand back in the apron pocket and fished out the telegram. She opened it with trembling hands. It was three short lines:

SIR GEORGE UNABLE TO SEND REQUESTED FUNDS STOP REMINDS MISS RUTHERFORD OF HER DEFIANCE AT THEIR LAST MEETING.

It was signed by some official in the British Parliament, a secretary of some kind.

Susan must have read the lines three or four times before the realization sank in.

The telegram had nothing to do with Mum.

It made no sense to Susan at all.

Susan refolded the telegram and stuffed it back into Bea's apron pocket. She hung the apron over the towel rack on the dry sink, and with her rags, she sopped up the spilled milk from the table. Then she grabbed the mop to tackle the floor. All the while her mind whirled.

Why on earth was Bea getting a telegram from the British Parliament?

Then, from some corner of Susan's memory, the words came floating back: *He was so stern, my grandfather was . . . He was a member of Parliament . . . We haven't spoken in years . . .*

The telegram was from Bea's grandfather.

↫

After dinner, Susan huddled with Helen in their bedroom, and Susan told her everything about the telegram and about Bea's feud with her grandfather.

"I'm stumped," Susan said. "If Bea asked her grandfather for money, she must be desperate. But I don't understand it—it seems like she has plenty. She spends it right and left. She even paid all our back rent as easy as buying a ticket to the picture show."

"Maybe that's it," said Helen. "Maybe the money she gave to Lester for our rent was all she had. I noticed her yesterday mending a hole in her stocking. She never used to do any mending. She'd just go out and buy a new pair."

"Yeah," said Susan. "Now that I think of it, those treats on Sunday were the first things she's splurged on in weeks. Yeah. Maybe Bea is out of money." She gnawed the inside of her lip, pondering. "But she wouldn't wire her grandfather for plain old spending money. There's too much bad blood between them. Bea must need money for something really important."

"But what, Susie?" Helen whispered.

Susan was grim. "I wonder if it has something to do with Mum. All I can guess is that the money Bea needs has something to do with Mum coming home."

Helen's eyes widened. "Do you think Mum's being held for ransom?"

Susan shook her head. "Poor people like us don't get kidnapped for ransom. I'm thinking it's something else." Susan felt a sudden burning in her chest as a thought occurred to her. "You know what I think, Helen? *I* think it has something to do with Bea's secret."

Helen's mouth dropped open. "Bea's secret! I forgot all about it. But how could her romance have anything to do with Mum?"

"I don't think her secret *is* a romance. And I don't think it's a spy mission either. I don't know what Bea's secret is, but I have a feeling it might be wrapped up in *all* of this—the fight with her grandfather, Mum's disappearance, the telegram, *everything*." Susan stood up and peered down at Helen on the bed. "We've got to find that letter with the secret in it, Helen—tonight."

"But you can't just go snooping in her room. That's . . . not right."

"Is it right for Bea to lie to us about where Mum is?" Susan asked.

Helen gave a troubled sigh. "No, I guess not."

Susan was sorry to put it so bluntly, but she had to make Helen understand. Like it or not, they could no longer trust Bea.

"You'll have to get Bea out of the house somehow," Susan told Helen, "so I can search her room." The girls decided that Helen would ask Bea to take her to the Girl Scout meeting. Susan would beg off, saying she had too much homework. Bea and Helen would be gone at least an hour, Susan figured. After she got Lucy in bed, Susan should still have plenty of time to scour Bea's room for the letter.

Susan waited for ten minutes after Lucy was tucked in to be perfectly sure that Bea and Helen were well on their way to the Hudson Guild. She crept into Bea's room and carefully stepped over the creaky floorboard in front of the door. From the nightstand, Bea's clock ticked out a warning to *hur-ry, hur-ry, hur-ry*. Susan stood by the nightstand, forcing herself to breathe evenly. Then she reached for the handle of the drawer and gently, gently pulled it out. Inside, Susan found Bea's reading glasses, a pair of silk gloves, a box of hairpins, and a stack of embroidered handkerchiefs.

No letter.

Susan groaned. She should have known Bea wouldn't leave the letter in the drawer where Susan had seen her place it. Bea probably moved it the first chance she had to a more secure hiding place.

But where?

Someplace inaccessible, maybe a jewelry box, something with a lock. Yet, to Susan's knowledge, Bea had no jewelry box. She kept her brooches on the dresser. The only other jewelry she had was a locket with her mother's picture, which she wore all the time. Bea's trunk was full of clothes and hats, and it wasn't locked anyway. There was really no place to hide anything.

Where then? Where should she look? The clock seemed to tick more loudly than ever, making Susan aware that minutes were slipping by while she wavered.

She'd just have to start. Anywhere. The dresser was as good a place as any. Her knees wobbly and her heart hammering, she pulled out the top drawer. Bea's underclothes. Stockings and chemises and bloomers. She lifted each garment in turn, felt among its folds for the letter, and then replaced it exactly as Bea had had it.

She checked each drawer in the same careful way, feeling more and more tense as the letter failed to appear. The bottom drawer was the heaviest, and it had always stuck, so Susan yanked hard at it—too hard. The drawer jerked loose from its runners and toppled out.

Susan stared, not believing what she saw under the dresser where the drawer had been: a rectangular package wrapped in brown paper and tied with string. She could guess what was inside that package, for it was wrapped just the way it had been when Bea pulled it out of her trunk on the night she arrived.

It had to be the Trafalgar Square photograph.

Susan picked up the package. She loosened the strings and let the brown paper fall to the floor. The frame looked even more richly burnished than it had the first time she'd seen it. Susan pictured Bea polishing the dark wood; she pictured her wrapping the frame and placing it gently under the dresser, then sliding the drawer in on top of it. Bea had obviously gone to great lengths to hide this photograph.

Why?

Susan studied every detail in the photograph for a clue. Something was nagging at her brain . . . something. Then she had it: the girl standing next to Bea looked like a much younger Alice Paul, the stirring speaker at the suffrage rally.

Susan wanted to be sure, so she slid the photograph out of the frame to have a closer look.

And then, right into her lap, as if inviting itself to be read, dropped the letter. Bea's letter.

The *secret* letter.

Tick-tick, tick-tick, went the clock. A horn beeped down in the street. Susan's pulse beat in her throat. She unfolded the letter and began to read.

She skimmed over the first couple of paragraphs—about doings of people Susan assumed were friends of Bea's and the writer's. When Susan's eyes fell on the third paragraph, her heart began to pound. The writer was asking Bea to come to America to help with "our cause."

Goose bumps rose on her skin as Susan read again the familiar line: "Your work must be kept secret for now." What? What was the work that Bea was to do?

Susan's eyes raced on, searching for the answer. "We want an appearance of strength," the writer went on, "not division, and there are those among us, even among our leaders, who wouldn't approve of what you're doing. There will be time for full disclosure later. When we've achieved our goal, no one will question our methods."

No one will question our methods. It sounded so grim.

Then Susan glanced at the signature, and a chill ran down her spine. The letter was signed simply "Alice." But Susan could supply the last name—Paul.

The writer of Bea's letter was Alice Paul.

And the "cause" Alice Paul mentioned was the suffrage movement.

So Bea was a suffragist. Well, that did explain some things. Like Bea's argument with Mum over Kathleen's stand on suffrage. It also explained Bea's injuries Saturday night. She got them at the suffrage rally.

But the letter left even more questions *un*answered. What was the work Bea was doing for suffrage that had to be kept secret? And what did it have to do with Mum?

Susan wracked her brain for any detail that might help her make a connection between Bea's secret and Mum. She thought back to the night Mum disappeared. She remembered Bea hobbling in, walking past Susan and Helen with scarcely a hello, and she remembered thinking it was strange that Bea didn't comment on Mum's absence.

Then Bea had been so reluctant to let Susan into her room. That heavy sigh, as if Susan was a bother. Her eagerness for Susan to leave. And the way she had turned her photograph away from Susan's view.

Why? Susan thought. *Why did Bea try to keep me from looking at that photograph?*

She couldn't have known Susan was at the suffrage rally. Maybe Bea was afraid Susan had seen Alice Paul's picture in the newspaper and would recognize her as one of Bea's friends in the photograph.

Why, though, would Bea want to hide her friendship with Alice Paul? It came back somehow, Susan was sure, to Bea's letter and her secret work for suffrage. But the more Susan's thoughts went round and round, the more confused she felt. She didn't see how Bea's letter could have anything to do with Mum. Whatever Bea was doing for suffrage, surely Mum would have no part in it. She had seen what had happened to Kathleen.

Which meant Bea's secret had led Susan nowhere.

CHAPTER 10
TRACKING DOWN MUM

 The black iron railings of the fire escape blocked Susan's view from her bedroom window. She had to lean out to see the trains that rumbled by on the Grand Central Overpass, and even further out to see the steamers and tugboats that pulled through the dark, restless waters of the Hudson.

Susan spent most of the night leaning out the window, watching the life of the city below. She couldn't sleep. She felt dark and restless like the Hudson—and lonely. She wondered if Mum was somewhere out there in the ever wakeful city, missing Susan as much as Susan missed her.

Susan finally grew sleepy as the pink light of morning washed the last faint stars from the sky. She crawled back in bed next to Helen and Lucy. The last sound she heard before she drifted off to sleep was the rattle of the milk wagon across the cobblestone street below.

The next thing she knew, Helen was jostling her. "Wake up, Susie. Lenny Rubenstein is here, in the kitchen. He says there's a phone call for you at the drugstore."

Susan struggled to consciousness through a black fog. Then her head cleared. Lenny's family owned the corner drugstore, and they had the only telephone on the block.

"Bea left early this morning, but she said to let you sleep till the last minute, and it's seven o'clock now. Breakfast is on the table, and Lenny's waiting to let you in the store."

Susan was up now and pulling on her clothes. *Mum—it had to be Mum on the telephone.* Who else would be calling her? Susan didn't even know anyone with a telephone.

"Hurry, Susie," Helen said. "I'll watch Lucy. Lenny's waiting for you."

෯

Susan followed Lenny to the drugstore. The phone was in the back, in the little room where Mr. Rubenstein mixed his medicines. She picked up the receiver, her nerves strung tight. "Hello?"

"Susan?" The quavery voice was one Susan didn't recognize.

"This is Susan."

"'Tis your Aunt Blanche. I'm sorry to be calling you so early, lass, but I've been distressed, I have, since I got your telegram last night. I got a ride into town this morning and roused poor Mr. Rucker from his bed to use his telephone. I haven't seen nor heard from your ma in over a year, not since your dad's funeral. Is she missing then?"

Susan's tongue would barely work. "She told us she was going to visit you on Saturday. We haven't seen her since."

"And you didn't notify the police because you were thinking she was here." She paused. "You poor girls, all alone in that city. I'll be on the first train out this morning."

"No need for that." Susan's voice came out wooden. What could her frail old Aunt Blanche possibly do to help them? "We're not alone. There's a boarder staying with us. She's taking care of us."

As soon as the words were out of her mouth, Susan shivered. Bea taking care of them? Hardly. She'd been lying to them since the day she arrived.

As Susan hung up the phone, an even more chilling thought struck her. Aunt Blanche said she hadn't heard from Mum in over a year, but Mum had told the girls that Aunt Blanche *asked* her to visit.

That meant that Mum had lied to them, too.

Sick with that realization, Susan dragged out of the drugstore, climbed the battered steps to the fourth-floor

landing, and dragged down the long, dreary hallway to
their flat.

She found Helen with her arms plunged in dishwater.
Helen turned as Susan came in. "I washed up the dishes
so you wouldn't have to, Susie, and took Lucy to the
Cochrans'. Who was that on the telephone?" Her voice
was both eager and anxious.

Susan told Helen about her conversation with Aunt
Blanche. After she finished, Helen was very still. Through
the open window, Susan was aware of traffic moving in the
street below—automobiles, delivery wagons, a coal truck
rumbling by.

"What do we do now?" Helen asked. Susan could see
in Helen's eyes the same dread she felt.

"We're not going to school," Susan said firmly. "We
have to find out where Mum went on Saturday morning—
whether she was headed for the train station or somewhere else."

"But Mum's the only one who could tell us that."

"Maybe not. Maybe someone saw Mum that morning
and could tell us at least which way she was walking. That
would give us a place to start, anyway."

"There's tons of people who could've seen her. We
can't possibly ask them all."

"No, but we can ask the one person who knows everything that happens on 26th Street."

"Mrs. Flynn," said Helen.

⸙

Mrs. Flynn invited the girls in with only a mild look of surprise on her face. She didn't even ask them why they weren't in school. The Flynn kitchen, though identical to the O'Neals' kitchen one floor below, looked half the size with so many people stuffed into it. Four of the Flynn boys were on the floor playing with blocks of wood. One of the twins was crawling on the floor chasing dust balls. Baby Bridget was sleeping in a cradle in the corner. A woman in a flowered housedress stood over a large wooden bowl peeling carrots and plunking them into a pot bubbling on the stove. Her complexion was as red as Mrs. Flynn's. She looked, in fact, like a younger, thinner version of Mrs. Flynn.

"This is my sister Flossie from Boston," said Mrs. Flynn. "She's been telling me for months she was coming to visit. She finally decided to make good on her word." Mrs. Flynn's eyes were dancing as she returned to a pile of potatoes she was paring at the table.

Flossie wiped her hands on a dishrag and greeted the girls. "Bertie's been promising to take me to meet the neighbors, but she's kept me so busy whisking me around town, I've scarce had a chance to meet anyone."

The last thing Susan wanted to do was chat, but she swallowed her impatience and tried to be polite. "When did you arrive?" she asked.

Mrs. Flynn answered for her sister, peeling all the while. The knife in her hand flew, shaving curly skins that dropped—*plunk*—into the metal garbage pail at her side. "She came in Saturday on the 6 A.M. And I was at the station at five to pick her up. Those train schedules are never accurate, as you lassies know, and I wasn't having my baby sister sitting alone at that station waiting for me."

Flossie was saying something, but Susan didn't hear her. *If Mum had been telling the truth about going to the train station on Saturday morning, then Mrs. Flynn might have seen her there.*

Susan exchanged glances with Helen, and she could tell Helen was thinking the same thing. Susan's heart was beating so loudly she could hardly hear herself speak. "You didn't happen to run into our mother, did you, Mrs. Flynn? At the station?"

"I didn't, lass. I must have missed her. Her friends arrived on the 6 A.M., too, did they?"

Susan thought she must have heard wrong. "I'm not sure what you mean, Mrs. Flynn."

"Why, the friends we saw your mother with at Hearn's." Hearn's was a huge department store on 14th Street that had a café inside and a fountain in the entry. "I thought you were saying she picked them up at the station on Saturday morning." Peelings fell one after another into the pail. *Plunk, plunk, plunk.*

Susan struggled to speak. "You saw Mum at Hearn's? When?"

"Let me see . . ." Mrs. Flynn scratched her double chin. "I showed Flossie the Grand Opera House first, on 23rd; then we went to Macy's. What time was it, Flossie, when we got to Hearn's? Around ten?"

"Aye, I think so." Flossie turned to Susan. "Your ma was sitting at a fancy table in the café, having tea with her friends, I'm remembering."

Mrs. Flynn picked up the story. "She acted startled to see me, she did, then like she barely knew me. If I didn't know your mum, I'd have thought she was ashamed of me. What was she doing with those hoity-toity society women, anyway? That one lady had her pug dog dressed in a sweater and was feeding it cake, like 'twas a person. I've never seen the like." Mrs. Flynn sniffed and threw a peeling into the pail—hard, as if for emphasis. It thumped against the side of the pail.

The sound echoed in Susan's head. *A pug dog with a sweater.* An intense pressure was building in her chest. That was *Bea's* society woman, the one Susan had seen her with at the post office. It had to be.

Suddenly Susan felt weak in the knees. She was short of breath, and she could barely force words out of her mouth. "Well, Mrs. Flynn," she managed. "We have to be going. We've got some things we need to do for Mum."

Helen followed Susan's lead. "A pleasure meeting you,

Miss Flossie." Helen always remembered her manners, even when Susan didn't.

"We'll come again when we can stay," Susan added, hurrying Helen out the door.

"Aye, do that," called Mrs. Flynn after them, "and bring your mum with you."

The slam of the door bounced off the green, blistered walls of the hall. Helen started to speak. "Shhh," Susan said, and took her by the hand to the stairway landing. Through the small window, smudged with dirt, they had a foggy view of the clutter of wash poles and fences in the yard five stories below.

Helen looked as if she was about to cry. "Susie?" Helen's voice quivered. "Where *is* Mum? Will she ever come home?"

Helen looked so small and forlorn, a wave of protectiveness washed over Susan. "Sit down, sweetie," she said. She pulled Helen down onto the top stair and hugged her close. "Of course Mum will come home," she promised, trying, for Helen's sake, to sound confident. Inside, all Susan felt was uncertainty . . . and fear. She hugged Helen tighter.

At that moment there was a scuffling sound on one of the landings below—someone coming up the stairs. From the top of the stairwell where the girls sat, there was a clear view straight down to the foyer. They could see a hat ascending the first flight of stairs—someone wearing a hat, a brimless one with huge lavender silk flowers. Susan recognized the hat; it was one of Bea's.

Susan turned to Helen and put her fingers to her lips. "Don't move," she mouthed. If they scrambled now to get out of sight, Bea was certain to see them. If they sat very quietly *and* if Bea didn't happen to glance up, maybe she wouldn't notice them.

Susan needn't have worried. Bea didn't glance right or left, up or down, as she came up the stairs. She was shuffling, moving very slowly, just like she had last Saturday night. And she was talking to herself, mumbling, though Susan couldn't make out anything she said. Susan even heard a funny, strangled sound she thought might be a sob. Helen must have heard the same thing; she shot Susan an anxious look. Susan practically held her breath as Bea paused at the landing and fumbled in her pocket for her key.

Don't let her look up, don't let her look up, Susan prayed.

Then Bea moved out of sight, into the twilight of the fourth-floor hall. Her footsteps thudded down the hall, slow and heavy—then stopped. Susan listened for the door to close. At last, she heard it. Bea was inside the flat.

Susan sighed. The tension drained from her muscles, partly because Bea hadn't seen them, mostly because she had reached a decision about what she was going to do.

"Did you hear Bea crying?" Helen asked. Her voice brimmed with concern. "I wonder what was the matter with her."

"I don't know." Susan purposely made her voice hard. "I don't care right now. I'm fed up with Bea. There's no doubt in my mind now that Bea knows something about Mum's disappearance. And it's clear Bea's not going to tell us what she knows. So I've thought of another way to get the truth from her."

"How, Susie?"

"I'll let her lead me to it. When she comes out of our flat, I'm going to follow her."

CHAPTER 11

BEA'S JOB

Susan rushed down the stairs to the street and hurried to the corner, careful to stay out of sight should Bea happen to glance out the window onto 26th Street. Susan had told Helen to go to the Cochrans' and wait. She was afraid it would be too conspicuous for both of them to try to trail Bea. Susan lingered at the drugstore, pretending to look at postcards, for what seemed like a very long time. Finally she saw Bea come out of the tenement and turn toward Ninth Avenue. Susan couldn't believe her luck; Bea was still wearing that outlandish hat. She would be easy to follow. Careful to keep her distance, Susan dogged Bea down the avenue twelve blocks to 14th Street.

This was Chelsea's business district, lined with office buildings and fancy department stores. Macy's was here, A.T. Stewart's, and Hearn's. Bea disappeared into a tall building with arched windows. Susan, waiting outside, measured the seconds. If she followed too soon, Bea might see her; if she waited too long, she would lose Bea entirely. Susan waited as long as she dared, then ducked inside, but it was too late. There was no sign of Bea in the foyer or on the staircase. Bea must have taken the elevator.

Susan stuck her head through the bars of the elevator cage. "Did a woman go up just now?" she asked the attendant. He was wearing a red and black uniform and white gloves.

"I take women up all day long," the man sniffed.

"This woman had a British accent. And a funny-looking lavender hat."

"Ah, yes, that woman went to the tenth floor, I believe."

"Can you take me there, please?"

"That's my job."

The operator closed the bars and pulled a lever. The elevator jerked upward, and Susan watched the floors speed by. Finally the elevator reached Floor Number 10.

Susan stepped out into a long hall lined with doors. How would she ever figure out which room Bea had entered?

Then Susan saw that most of the doors had name-plates. Down the hall she went, scanning the plates for something that might tell her which door was the right one. *Lloyd and Lloyd, Attorneys-at-law. Schneider and Sons. Jeffrey P. Whitehead, Accountant.* And then she saw it—*Committee for Woman Suffrage!*

With a mixture of apprehension and excitement, Susan pushed the door open a crack and peered in. The reception room was empty, but she heard voices coming from an inner office behind a door that was slightly ajar. The voices were female, all of them. One she recognized. It was Bea.

Susan stepped into the reception room and closed the door behind her. Now she could hear most of the conversation, but she couldn't figure out what the women were talking about. Something about some friends of theirs who were in trouble. Then Susan realized—they were discussing the suffragists who'd been arrested at the rally and jailed.

"The organization is getting valuable publicity from this," someone said. "We used to get scarcely a mention in the papers. Now we're on the front page every day."

"And it's favorable publicity. People are outraged at the way our women are being treated by the authorities. Tammany Hall charging them with inciting a riot and trying to slap long prison sentences on them—it's ridiculous," said someone else.

"And it's not that our sisters aren't willing to serve prison time for the cause," said a third voice. "You know they are; we've all done it before. It's just so encouraging to see that the citizens of New York are on *our* side. People see the Tammany bosses as the underhanded villains they are."

Then Susan heard Bea speak. "Yes, yes, the publicity will help us—that's clear." Susan thought she heard impatience in Bea's voice. "But a problem's arisen from the rally—a serious problem."

Bea sounded so grave and so urgent, Susan wondered what kind of problem she could be talking about. She strained to hear what Bea would say next.

"You remember the friend I told you about," Bea went on, "the one who had so much potential for aiding the cause?"

A chorus of voices rose in acknowledgment; yet, over the noise, Susan could hear her heart pounding against her chest. Was Bea talking about Mum?

Bea continued slowly, as if each word were painful to pronounce. "We were near the front of the crowd when the violence broke out. In the commotion, we got separated, and I lost sight of her in the crowd. I was pushing forward to find her when I was set upon by a policeman with a club, and I took a nasty beating before I could break away. By then, my friend had completely disappeared. When I couldn't find her after the crowd dispersed, I was certain she'd been arrested and carted away to jail, but—"

Jail! Mum arrested and taken to jail.

The room began closing in on Susan. Her throat felt tight. Suddenly all the scattered pieces that had made no sense fell together in Susan's mind. The mysterious bits of conversation between Mum and Bea. Mum's reaction to Kathleen's being fired and the argument over Kathleen's stand on suffrage. Bea's urging Mum to "do more for us." Mum's strange meeting with the society ladies at Hearn's. And most telling of all, the connection between Bea's letter and Mum's disappearance.

Susan couldn't bear to stay in the room one minute longer. Fighting the urge to run, she crept out of the room, but the outer door creaked as she closed it.

"Who's there?" one of the voices called from the inner office.

Panicking, Susan fairly jumped into the hall and tripped over a loose floor tile. She was on her feet in an instant. Behind her, she heard Bea calling her name. She hesitated, only for a second, but that was long enough for Bea to catch up with her.

"What are you doing here?" Bea asked. Her expression was pained.

"Maybe I should ask you the same question," Susan flung back. "This isn't the Nabisco factory, is it, Bea?"

"I can explain that—"

"With more of your lies?"

Bea looked stricken. "Susan, I had to have a cover for my work. You don't understand the opposition we're up against, from blokes like Lester Barrow. I couldn't very well pop into your flat and announce I was here to organize your neighborhood for suffrage."

"Hold on. What do you mean?"

"We need the working class, Susan. We can't win the vote without their support. The movement's been upper and middle class until now, and it's failed. We need the masses, the immigrants, the working people. And the working class will only listen to their own.

"That's why I was sent to find someone to lead them from their own class—like your mother—to win them over. Me, a blue-blooded Brit, they'd never listen to. So I needed to go among you, with a cover, until I could find those leaders. Working at the factory was my cover. I wouldn't have lied to you without reason, Susan."

Susan's mind was a jumble; she was trying to comprehend what Bea was saying to her, but all she could think about was the anguish Bea had put her through. "What was your reason for lying about where Mum was?"

A look of distress flashed across Bea's face, and Susan read guilt in Bea's eyes. Susan blinked back sudden tears. Deep down, against all the evidence, a part of her had kept on hoping that Bea's deceptions would somehow turn out to be a simple mistake. Now Bea's guilty face had destroyed that hope.

Bea opened her mouth to say something, but Susan stopped her. "Just tell me one thing, Bea. Where is my mother?" Susan knew the answer now, but she wanted to hear Bea say it. To hear Bea tell her the truth just once.

Bea was silent for a long time. When she finally

answered, her voice was quiet and small. "Oh, Susan, I don't know where she is."

Another lie. Susan's throat ached. "I heard what you said in there. About what happened to Mum. You've done nothing but lie to us since the day you came." Now the tears were coming fast, and Susan didn't try to hold them back. She turned and bolted for the stairs. She heard Bea calling her, but she didn't stop.

Susan didn't feel like going home, but she didn't know where else to go. Fourteenth Street was crammed now with shoppers, jostling and bumping and hurrying. Susan's head was pounding; she wanted time—and space—to think. She decided to head up 12th Avenue along the river. It was a longer walk, but the sidewalk wouldn't be so congested.

Once on 12th, Susan tried to gather her thoughts. There was no point to thinking more about Bea. The only thing that mattered was Mum. Susan hated the idea of Mum spending even one day in a stinking, rat-infested cell— much less weeks or even months. She had to think of a way to get Mum out of jail.

Susan knew she couldn't trust Bea to help her. Who else could she turn to? Aunt Blanche? The Cochrans? Mrs. Flynn? What could any of them do?

Across the street, Susan could see a band of river between two warehouses. A tugboat was butting through the water, leaving shimmery green ripples in its wake. On the other side of the river, she spied a patch of trees—the wooded hilltops of New Jersey. She had hazy memories of a long-ago ferry ride and a picnic there on the Jersey slopes. That was before Lucy was born, before Dad died, before Mum disappeared. Such happy memories seemed so distant it was as if they had happened to another person.

Tears prickled in Susan's eyes. She fought against the hopelessness that was settling on her. She couldn't give in to it. She had no one to depend on now but herself.

Susan stopped in her tracks. It was what Alice Paul had said in her speech! The words came back to Susan so forcefully now: *Sometimes a girl would have nothing but her own means to rely on.*

"But what means do I have?" Susan asked aloud.

Then it came to her. Her barbershop money! Why hadn't she thought of it sooner? She could use her own money to bail Mum out of jail!

It wasn't until Susan was down on her knees in her own bedroom, pulling her money out from the bureau drawer where she had hidden it, that it occurred to her she might not have enough to make the bail. When she counted it, the entire stash amounted to only five dollars and twenty-three cents. She couldn't imagine five dollars being enough to make bail.

Where could she get more money to add to her own?

Russell! He'd been saving much longer than Susan had, and he had two jobs. Hadn't he told her he had saved almost enough to buy a bicycle?

Susan found Russell at the barbershop on 28th Street. He protested when Susan pulled him away from a potential customer, a man in an expensive, double-breasted coat who Russell was sure would have been a big tipper. But when Susan told Russell what she had discovered, his eyes came alive and didn't once leave her face. She quickly filled him in on the whole story. He agreed to loan Susan as much money as she needed. "I know you'll pay me back. You're a good businessma—I mean woman." He grinned. "You going to let me come with you to the jail to spring your ma?"

ᕦ

It was two miles to the Police Central Headquarters on Centre Street, a long walk, but Susan didn't want to waste any of their precious money on carfare. She and Russell headed south by way of Fifth Avenue, through Greenwich Village, then down Broadway to the edge of Little Italy.

There, on a block of seedy, run-down tenements, some barefoot children on a stoop stared at Russell and Susan as they walked past. A woman stuck her head out the window and screamed at the children in a language Susan didn't understand. They scattered and joined the hordes of children playing in the street.

"Only a few more blocks to Centre Street," Russell told Susan. Russell had been to Police Central once with his father to bail his Uncle Timothy out of jail.

Sure enough, as soon as they turned on to Broome Street, Susan saw the dome of the headquarters rising majestically above the clutter of tenements and shabby buildings in the neighborhood. It looked like a cathedral, Susan thought, or a palace—not a jail.

Susan's throat closed at the idea of Mum imprisoned behind those stone walls. Would Mum be wearing a ball and chain and a striped uniform like the "jailbirds" Susan had seen in movies? She shuddered at the thought, and Russell quietly put his hand on her shoulder. "Do you want me to go in alone and bail her out?" he asked.

Susan set her jaw. "No, I can handle it." She looked straight ahead as they climbed the granite steps of the building, and kept her mind focused on having Mum home again.

Inside, Susan found herself in a huge rotunda with marbled walls and a marble staircase winding up to a landing above. At a massive desk in the middle of the rotunda sat a very large officer with a very sour look on his face.

Every ounce of courage drained from Susan's body. For an instant she feared she could never approach that desk, but she made herself think of Alice Paul's words—*rely on yourself*—and her courage returned. She told the officer what she wanted.

He looked at his ledger. "Ain't no one by that name in this jail," he said.

"No, but there is," Susan insisted. "She's my mother. I know she's here. Rose O'Neal."

"What? You think I can't read? This is my roster, and there ain't no Rose O'Neal on it," he growled.

"Could you check one more time?" asked Russell. "Maybe you missed her name."

"Look! I don't need a couple of kids telling me my business. Beat it. I got work to do."

Susan's brain froze. She couldn't think. She could hardly move. *Where in the name of heaven was Mum?* It was all she could do to go back down the granite steps. On the last step she collapsed. She felt like crying, but she wouldn't dare give in to the urge—not in front of Russell. He sat down beside her and put his hand on her knee. He didn't say anything, just pushed around some pebbles with the toe of his shoe. After a long time, he spoke. "Are you sure it was your mum Bea was talking about?"

"Yes, I'm sure. It had to be." Susan could no longer hold back the tears. One slid down her cheek and dropped onto her knee beside Russell's hand. He pulled his handkerchief from his pocket and handed it to Susan. She swiped her cheek with it. "Mum can't just have disappeared into thin air. She *has* to be somewhere, doesn't she?"

"Of course she does, Sue. I suppose there *are* other jails in this city, but it seems like they'd have brought the suffragists here, don't you think?"

Susan didn't answer. Her heart had nearly stopped at her own words. People *did* disappear into thin air—in this city they did. Like the dockworkers Dad knew who had angered Lester Barrow.

Lester Barrow!

Suddenly the blood pounded through Susan's head and rammed against her skull. Mum, arrested as a suffragist . . . She would have done anything to keep people like Lester Barrow and Mr. Riley from finding out. She would have tried to hide her arrest any way she could, wouldn't she? Now Susan was sure she knew what had happened. Her words tumbled one over the other as she explained to Russell: Mum had given a false name when she was arrested!

"Maybe that's it, Susan. But what name would she have used?" Russell asked. "Her maiden name?"

Susan shook her head. "Mum's family was German— Protestant, you know. They disowned her when she married Dad. She won't even talk about them. Besides, with the war in Europe now, nobody likes Germans. She'd have given the jailer her own name before she called herself 'Rosa Ullman.'"

"Then what name would she have used?" Russell asked.

Susan could think of only one possibility—"Lillian,"

the name Mum had dreamed of using for her vaudeville career. She explained to Russell.

"Just 'Lillian.' No last name?"

"I don't know what last name she would've used. She always just said 'Lillian'."

"We're supposed to bail out every Lillian listed on the jailhouse roster?"

"Doesn't look like we have any other choice."

Russell's jaw worked back and forth. After a long silence, he admitted that Susan was right. "I guess it's back inside then?"

"I guess so," said Susan.

The officer grimaced when he saw them. "I thought I told you two your ma wasn't here."

"We want you to check your list again," Susan said, "this time for a Lillian."

"Oh, your mother's changed her name, has she? Or is Lillian your grandmother?"

"Please, just check the list," said Russell.

The officer grumbled, but he pulled out the ledger. Susan waited tensely as she watched his eyes move back and forth across the roster. "What'd you say the last name was?" he asked.

Did that mean he had a Lillian?

Susan swallowed. If she acted unsure of the name, maybe he wouldn't tell her anything. She would have to fake it. She glanced quickly at Russell, bidding him to follow her lead. His eyes met hers, and she was sure he understood. "Well, sir, we didn't say actually. You see, we haven't seen our mother in a very long time, and we wondered whether she was dead. Now we find out she's alive, but we're not sure what her last name is . . . now."

"She might have gotten married again," said Russell. "Do you have a Lillian?" He craned his neck to try to see the list.

The jailer looked annoyed. "The only Lillian I have here is Lillian Murphy. Now is that your ma or ain't it?"

Doubt tormented Susan. Was this person really Mum? Or a total stranger? "Can't we see her?" Susan asked.

"Sorry. No visitors allowed. Orders from city hall."

Susan was torn. What if they used all their money paying bail for Lillian Murphy, and she wasn't even Mum?

"Our mother might have been a suffragist," said Russell. "Do you know if this Lillian Murphy was arrested at the suffrage rally?"

"Does it look like I'm running a newspaper office? This is a jail. I'm not in the business of handing out information."

Susan pulled Russell aside to talk to him. "It's mostly your money," she said. "What d'you think?"

"I think the decision's up to you."

"But it's such a gamble—betting every penny we have on a hunch."

"Sometimes playing a hunch can be your best bet." His expression was intense.

Susan looked back at him with equal intensity. "Then let's play it," she said.

Chapter 12
Susan's Gamble

Susan paced the floor, her stomach in knots. She kept glancing nervously at the heavy door where the jail matron in her dark skirt and blouse had disappeared—the door that led to the cells. Any minute now the matron would return with someone using the name of Lillian Murphy, either Mum or a stranger who'd gotten lucky and been bailed out by two kids playing a hunch.

Finally Susan heard two sets of footsteps coming down the hall, one heavy, one light. Susan sucked in her breath, tried to prepare herself for anything, as the footsteps came closer. Then the door opened, and she saw Mum— her face strained and haggard—but Mum just the same.

Susan fell into her mother's arms.

❧

After so many days of tension and worry, it seemed too good to be true now to be walking through her own front door arm in arm with Mum.

Susan tried to stamp every detail of the moment into her mind, to convince herself that it was real. The way the sunlight streamed through the uncurtained top of the window and played against the kitchen wall. The faint odor of ammonia that always lingered in the kitchen. The apron hanging on the stove, and the old gray mop leaning in the corner. Best of all, Mum, at home again.

Mum was bruised and sore from being beaten at the rally. Russell helped Susan get Mum settled in the girls' bedroom. Then he went back to his flat to get Helen and Lucy.

Susan sat beside Mum on the bed and stroked her hair, like Mum always did when one of the girls was sick.

Mum smiled weakly. "Susie, my big girl." She clasped her fingers over Susan's hand. "I'm sorry to be such a troublemaker. I didn't intend to be. I had the idea I was getting into suffrage to help you girls. I didn't want to see you weighed down with the same kinds of problems I had."

Mum said she hadn't wanted to support suffrage openly for fear of what her boss or Lester Barrow would do. "I told Bea flat out I couldn't march in parades or do anything where I might be seen by someone who knew me, but I wanted to help. I was doing a lot of little things,

hoping they might add up to something that would make
a difference. I did some typewriting, sent out mailings.
Sometimes I'd go to neighborhoods where no one knew
me and take around petitions for people to sign. Even that
scared me, though. I was terrified that Lester or Mr. Riley
would find out and we'd find ourselves on the street. And
when Lester came by my office and demanded the back
rent, I was sure he suspected something. I told Bea I'd
have to quit the suffrage work.

"Well, Bea wouldn't hear of it. She insisted on using
her own money to pay Lester. She said it was worth it if
I felt a little more secure. And I did—until Kathleen was
fired."

For a minute Mum closed her eyes, and Susan saw the
gray shadows on her face. "That was like a rug pulled out
from under me. I felt like a fool for thinking there could
ever be security in this world for a poor widow with children
to feed. I told Bea I was through with suffrage."

That was the argument Susan had heard. The argument
that had started her worrying about Bea's secret.

Mum pushed herself up to a sitting position and
continued. "I thought that was the end of it, but a few
days later Bea came to me and said perhaps I wouldn't have
to work for Mr. Riley anymore. The suffrage organization
might have a job for me. They needed someone like me to
organize working-class neighborhoods for suffrage, and
they'd pay decent wages for the work.

"Bea said that a good friend of hers—a leader in the suffrage movement—was coming to town to speak at the rally on Saturday. Bea set up an interview for me with her friend and another suffrage leader on Saturday morning. By the end of the meeting, everything was arranged for me to take the job. I went off to the rally with such excitement. It seemed that I might really have some security at last." Mum's eyes brightened as she spoke, and Susan saw a spark of the old, unworried Mum, the before-Dad-died Mum. Susan thought wistfully how nice it would be to see that look on Mum's face more often.

Mum's eyes clouded as she went on with her story. "Of course, getting the interview with Bea's friend depended on my being off work on Saturday. Telling Mr. Riley the truth was out of the question after what happened to Kathleen, so I made up the story about visiting Aunt Blanche, who I said was near death. I figured I'd better tell you girls the same story lest you come by the office looking for me. I hated to lie to you, but I thought it was safer for us all—"

"Why didn't you at least tell me where you were going?" Susan said. "I would have kept your secret."

"I couldn't have burdened you with that. Suppose Lester Barrow had come by while you girls were there alone—"

Just then, the front door slammed, and Helen and Lucy pounded into the hall, shouting for Mum. They were on

Mum in a minute, hugging and kissing her. Lucy settled into Mum's lap and Helen snuggled up against Mum.

"Oh, I missed my girls," Mum said, smiling and hugging them close.

Susan was the first to see Bea, still wearing her brimless hat, appear in the doorway. Bea had an astonished look on her face. "Rose! You're . . . home." Her voice was trembling. "But how did you get here?"

The smile vanished from Mum's face. "Bea, didn't you know Susan had come to get me?"

Bea took a few hesitant steps into the room. "I didn't even know where you were, Rose. I had assumed you were in jail. I even wired my grandfather for money—I'd figured to bail you out, and I thought you might need to see a doctor, and I knew the rent was due, and—" Her chest heaved as though she was choking back a sob. "But my grandfather refused me the money. And when I went to the jail, they told me you weren't there. You can't imagine how frantic I was. I spent hours telephoning and running about the city, checking police stations and hospitals. Then I went down to suffrage headquarters, praying the leadership could help me find you."

Susan was breathing hard and fast. She had barely heard the rest of what Bea had said because she was stuck on the very first sentence. *Bea had been telling her the truth this morning!*

Mum was sitting on the edge of the bed now, looking

sheepish. "Oh, I was foolish, wasn't I? Making up a name to give the officers? All I was thinking about was Mr. Riley or Lester reading my name in the newspaper." Her expression changed to bewilderment, and she turned to look at Susan. "But Susie, if Bea didn't know where I was, then how did you know?"

Susan willed her voice to be steady. "I followed Bea to her suffrage headquarters and heard her telling her friends you'd been arrested. I—" she glanced at Bea—"left . . . before . . . before I heard the rest of what Bea said. Then Russell and I went to the jail and figured out about your name."

"What on earth possessed you to follow Bea?" Mum asked.

"Yes," Bea added, "I've been wondering that myself."

"You shouldn't have wondered, Bea!" Susan cried. "Did you think we were just dumb little kids, swallowing all those lies you were telling us?"

Then Susan couldn't talk fast enough. Bea and Mum listened without comment as Susan spilled out her story. She told them everything that had happened, all the way from her job at the barbershop to the girls' visit with Mrs. Flynn. When she finished, both Bea and Mum looked stunned.

Bea spoke first. "Susan, I don't know what to say. Except that I'm sorry. I thought I was sparing you from worry."

Bea took a small step toward Susan, then stopped.

Susan could feel Mum's eyes on her as well. Susan supposed they were waiting for her to say something, but she didn't—couldn't.

"Try to understand, Susan," Bea pleaded. "I was sick from worrying over your mother myself, and wanting so to shelter you girls—" Her voice broke, and she looked down.

Suddenly Susan remembered feeling just that way with Helen. This morning, on the landing. And earlier, at D'Attilio's Bakery, after Lester's threat. Both times, hadn't Susan been less than truthful with Helen, trying to shelter her from fear? *But those were little lies,* Susan told herself. *Not like Bea's.*

Bea had regained her composure. "I see now that I'd have frightened you less if I'd simply told you the truth. Why, Susan, you could even have helped solve the dilemma." Susan thought she heard pride in Bea's voice, and that made her heart ache, though she wasn't sure why.

"But I didn't." Bea sighed deeply. "I'm ignorant, not used to family matters, I'm afraid." She looked at Susan again and added softly, "I handled things badly, and I'm sorry. That's all I can say."

"And you needn't say anything else." Mum rose and put her hands on Bea's arms. "Part of being a family is understanding when we make mistakes. You did your best at the time." Mum's gaze swept to Helen and Lucy, then to Susan.

Helen and Lucy chorused their agreement. Lucy bounced across the bed and threw her arms around Bea's waist. Helen hugged Bea's neck.

Susan, gripped by a fierce burning in her chest, could only stand back and watch. She couldn't bring herself to enter in. Everyone else was so ready to forgive Bea, but Susan couldn't; she just couldn't. She felt like an outsider, and she turned toward the door.

"Susan," Mum called after her. "Where are you going?" There was concern on her face.

Susan looked back, and Bea's eyes caught hers. "Let me talk to her, Rose," said Bea.

Mum nodded. "We'll be right here."

Susan followed Bea into the other bedroom. Bea seated herself on the bed. She took off her hat and placed it next to her, then patted the bed on the other side of her. "Come sit, love."

Something inside of Susan wouldn't let her move toward Bea. She stood silently.

After a long moment, Bea's mouth trembled; then she closed her eyes and rubbed the bridge of her nose. When she opened her eyes, Susan noticed how bloodshot they were. "It was different between us, wasn't it, Susan? Different than it was with your mum or your sisters. We had a special friendship, you and I."

Yes! Susan's heart cried out. But all she could do was nod and swallow painfully.

Bea seemed to struggle for what she would say next. Finally she said, "I know you trusted me, Susan, and I failed you. I wish I could undo it. I wish I didn't have to see the hurt and disappointment in your eyes." She paused. "I felt that way about someone once. When I was about your age.

"You asked me before how I felt about my grandfather. You know I'd lived with him from the time my mother died, when I was quite small. I was so proud of that man, Susan. I wanted to be exactly like him. I told him so one day, when I was your age. Simply blurted it out at the dinner table. We didn't eat, you understand; we *dined*. Butlers and serving maids to wait on us. We had a huge mahogany table. I sat at one end and he at the other. And I wasn't allowed to speak unless he spoke to me first. Which he seldom did.

"I don't know why I broke the rule. I can't recall. For some reason, though, I blurted out there at the table that I wanted to be a member of Parliament someday, like him. I still remember the scowl that came over his face, and his voice, cold as ice, telling me, 'Females do not vote. Therefore they cannot serve in Parliament. Nor will they ever do so, as long as I have anything to do with it.' Then he went back to eating, without so much as a glance at me.

"I simply sat there at that big, long table, crying inside, but not daring to let him know how he'd hurt me. I never quite forgave him for that."

"Was that the argument you had with him?"

"Oh, no, that came much later. When I first became involved with the suffrage movement. My grandfather insisted I give it up, or he would cut me off financially. Of course I wouldn't, so he did. All I had after that was the money my mother left me, which I learned to live on quite comfortably."

Bea seemed absorbed for a moment in fingering the flowers on her hat. "What I'm trying to say, I suppose, is that you have to look to yourself, no one else, to make your dreams happen. That's really all we're fighting for with suffrage. The right of every human being to rely on him or herself."

Susan's skin tingled. *Alice Paul's words again.*

Susan ached to tell Bea how those words had helped her. She felt shy toward Bea, though, as if all the pain Bea caused her had raised a wall between them. She tried, haltingly, to put into words at least some of what was in her heart. "Bea? Your friend Alice Paul? If you see her again or write her, would you tell her I really liked her speech and what she said . . . what you just said . . . about relying on yourself. It's what got me through these last few days. It helped me . . . a lot. I'd just like her to know that."

Bea's eyes were shining. "That will mean quite a lot to Alice, Susan." Susan had the feeling it meant even more to Bea.

Bea rose, went to the dresser, slid open the heavy bottom drawer, then bent down and reached behind it. Susan's heart jumped. She knew Bea was retrieving the Trafalgar Square photograph. Bea turned back to Susan with the framed photograph clutched to her chest. "No secrets between us anymore, Susan." She looked at Susan earnestly. "I want you to have the photograph. Alice gave it to me, as a memento of the time we'd served together in Holloway Prison for our suffrage activities.

"Alice is a fighter, Susan, very determined, and she'll get what she wants in the end. We will get the vote, you'll see, and it'll be largely because of her. She's a good friend, whom I very much admire. I hope you'll remember what she stands for, and I hope someday you'll again think of me as a friend." She held the photograph out to Susan.

Into Susan's mind flooded all the many kindnesses Bea had performed since she came to live with them. Then Susan remembered what Bea had said to her that night on the roof when she was missing Dad so badly.

The best we can do with pain is to make something good come out of it.

Susan looked at Bea, still holding the framed photograph out to her. It would be a good thing, wouldn't it, to have a friend like Bea?

Susan smiled and reached out to take the photograph from Bea's hand.

"Are we friends, then?" Bea asked.

"Special friends." Whatever had been holding Susan back suddenly released her. She rushed forward into Bea's open arms.

1914

A Peek into the Past

LOOKING BACK: 1914

An ad against suffrage

By 1914, when Susan's story takes place, suffragists had been fighting for women's right to vote for more than 60 years. Suffragists had to battle the popular belief that women should tend to their homes and families, leaving politics and business to men. Some people even insisted that females were too emotional or not intelligent enough to be trusted with complex matters like government.

By the time of Susan's story, early suffrage leaders like Susan B. Anthony and Elizabeth Cady Stanton had given decades of their lives to the struggle. During the years these women worked for suffrage, the nation fought the Civil War, freed its slaves, and gave black men the right to vote with the Fifteenth Amendment to the Constitution. Anthony and Stanton worked tirelessly for an amendment giving women the vote, but Congress defeated it again and again. Eventually, a few western states allowed women to vote— Wyoming, Colorado, Utah, and Idaho—

Suffragists
Susan B. Anthony (top) and
Elizabeth Cady Stanton

but by the time Anthony died in 1906, not one state east of the Mississippi allowed women to vote. And much of the suffrage movement's fire seemed to die with Anthony.

Soon, though, a new generation of women—including Alice Paul—brought fresh energy to the suffrage movement. While studying in England from 1907 to 1910, Paul met the Pankhursts, a mother and her daughters who were setting England's suffrage movement ablaze.

Mrs. Pankhurst being taken to jail

The Pankhursts and their followers were called "the wild women of England" because they were willing to face arrest and jail to carry their message to the public. Some even resorted to throwing rocks and smashing windows. Many Pankhurst followers, including Alice Paul, served prison sentences. In jail, they endured mistreatment and pro-tested with hunger strikes.

Alice Paul didn't agree with every-thing the Pankhursts were doing, but she was inspired by their energy and by their success at drawing attention to suffrage. In America at that time, people barely

Many women served jail time for their suffrage work.

noticed the suffrage movement. In 1910, Alice Paul returned to the United States determined to change that.

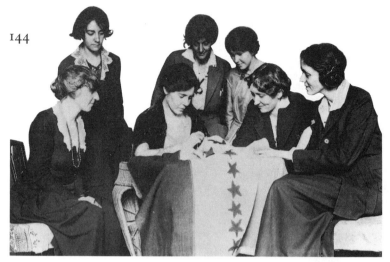

Alice Paul (third from left) sewing a suffrage flag

By then, most American suffragists had given up on changing the Constitution. Instead, they were trying to win the vote for women one state at a time. Alice Paul insisted there was a better, quicker way—passage of the Constitutional amendment Anthony and Stanton had fought for, guaranteeing *every* woman the right to vote.

Alice Paul and other young leaders used some of the Pankhursts' ideas to win support for the amendment. They held outdoor rallies and parades, carried signs, and gave speeches in public places.

Most suffragists, like these women, belonged to the upper or middle class.

And, for the first time, American suffragists looked beyond the wealthy and the middle class for support. Under Paul's leadership, they began to bring the movement to poor, working-class, and immigrant women, much as the fictional Bea Rutherford did.

Workers in a cigar factory

In large cities, poor families like the O'Neals—many of them immigrants—lived in ramshackle buildings called *tenements.* Large families lived in apartments of only two or three rooms. Thousands of people were crammed into a few blocks. Most, like Mum, needed jobs so desperately that they worked long hours under terrible conditions. Many took jobs in filthy, unsafe factories, often working 12 to 14 hours a day for less than a dollar.

Such neighborhoods were usually controlled by a *political machine*—a powerful group of local politicians much like Lester Barrow and his men. Such men, called *political bosses,* had great influence over the poor, uneducated people who lived in their districts. Political bosses helped families in

New York City tenements in the early 1900s

Tammany Hall and
a political boss

times of sickness and trouble, but they expected absolute loyalty in return. People were thrown out of their homes and jobs if they displeased the bosses, just as Mum's friend Kathleen was. New York City had the most famous political machine in America. It was called *Tammany Hall,* after the building where the political bosses met. For years political machines in major cities opposed suffrage. They feared that women voters might limit their power or even vote them out of office.

Alice Paul not only brought the suffrage movement into tenements and factories, she also made the White House take

notice. In 1913, Paul organized a huge parade to take place in Washington, D.C., on the day that President Woodrow Wilson took office. The parade ended in a riot, and the police refused to help the suffragists, just as Susan experienced at the rally she attended. The event made headlines across the country.

Suffrage parade in
Washington, D.C., in 1913

American suffrage was getting noticed at last.

Over the next few years, suffragists gained more and more attention. They staged parades and rallies in every state. They picketed, carried signs, collected names on petitions, spoke in lecture halls and on street corners—wherever they could get someone to listen. Sometimes they were arrested and jailed, but like

A suffragist speaker

Mum, they came out even more determined to win their rights. The national organizations that worked for suffrage grew by leaps and bounds, counting among their members men and women from all walks of life. The cry "Votes for Women" echoed in towns and cities all across America.

Finally, in 1918 President Wilson decided to support the suffrage amendment. He helped convince other law-makers that the time had come to grant women the vote. On August 26, 1920, the Nineteenth Amendment was signed into law, giving women full rights as United States citizens.

Yet Alice Paul and other suffrage leaders knew the fight for women's equality had only begun. Perhaps someday American girls could not only look forward to voting for president, they could even hope to *be* president.

Women proudly casting their first votes

ABOUT THE AUTHOR

Elizabeth McDavid Jones has lived most of her life in North Carolina. She grew up sandwiched between two brothers. She used to wish she were a boy because she thought boys got to have more fun than girls. One of her earliest dreams was to be a jockey in the Kentucky Derby—but only men were allowed to do that. Today, she lives with her husband and four children in Greenville, North Carolina.